ARCHIBALD'S AUNT

John McDermott

TSL Publications

First published in Great Britain in 2020
By TSL Publications, Rickmansworth

Cover image: Duncan Bourne

ISBN / 978-1-913294-45-8

For Marjorie

1

Archie stopped the car and peered through the splattered windscreen at the scene ahead. It wasn't an encouraging sight. After driving all day, the last thing he needed was for his journey to end in a lane covered in mud and potholes. Okay if you were driving one of those off-road affairs, but not for the old banger that had struggled to get him this far. He switched off the engine and lights and climbed out into the darkness. The rain had stopped but the air was cold. He decided that rather than risk being marooned in the mud, it would be better to abandon the car and his luggage and walk the rest of the way.

After the noise of the city, this was a tranquil sort of place, disturbed only by the occasional small animal making its way through the undergrowth or the hoot of an owl somewhere in the distance. But for most of the time, there was only the soothing sound of water as it trickled its way over the weir on the nearby river. Pausing for a moment to enjoy the peace, he tried to remember how much further there was to go. Perhaps no more than a few hundred yards, but far enough when you had to find your way through mud on a night made dark by heavy cloud.

Progress wasn't easy. Slipping and sliding without anything to hang on to, he just about managed to stay upright until he stuck his foot into the middle of a pothole and cold water shot up his leg. As he teetered about, his mood darkened and he roundly cursed dark country lanes, potholes, hooting owls, the rain, and everything else that was keeping him out of a warm bed on a chilly autumn night.

He stumbled on, eventually spotting a light over to his left as his hand encountered the top of a low fence. Finally, he'd arrived at the front garden of the cottage. Feeling his way along, he came to the familiar wooden gate and pushed it open, causing the hinges to give out a loud groan. It was a déjà vu moment. Years on and the rusty metal still awaited that soothing spot of oil.

Inside the garden he paused. As a boy he'd spent many long summer weeks here with his mother's sister, Ruby, who was married to Fred, a sergeant in the police. When his father's job had taken the family to America, he'd missed home and the holidays spent in this part of the English countryside. He felt especially bad when news reached him that Fred had died, leaving Ruby on her own in the isolated cottage. That decided him. He'd get back as soon as possible to surprise her and offer his support. Now, having finally arrived at the old place he was looking forward to his stay.

The light from the cottage window was low and flickering. 'Great,' he thought, 'she's still using oil lamps!' Not as convenient as switching on electric lights of course but totally in keeping with the ambience of the place. He was roused from these thoughts when it started to rain again.

The glimmer from the window did little to light the surroundings but he was confident he knew the garden well. He moved quickly along the path, his mind occupied with thoughts of a warm welcome, a hot drink and a seat by the fire in the big living room.

He hardly noticed the ground under his feet no longer had the feel of a garden path and progress was becoming difficult. Eventually, as the building loomed up in front of him, he reached out a hand and felt the rugged stone of the old place. He paused to enjoy a moment of relief that he'd finally made it.

He moved cautiously on and so focused was he on reaching the door, that he failed to notice before him the stick-like object that rested against the cottage wall. This was brought to his attention as he took his next step and something hard and unyielding leapt out of nowhere that struck him a resounding blow on the head. What followed seemed to happen almost in slow motion. For a split second he remained upright, before executing a sort of half pirouette and falling flat on his face into the nearby flowerbed. He landed with a thud and immediately felt as if someone was sticking pins into his legs. His mouth opened and a loud yell escaped it before his face buried itself in soft mud. The noise caused an immediate stir inside the cottage.

There was a scrambling sound, a lock scraped and the noise of bolts being drawn before the door flew open. Light illuminated the scene and through the opening shot a small female figure exuding outrage. She was carrying some sort of weapon in one hand. 'All right!' she yelled. 'The game's up. Come on out with your hands up!'

Archie was in no mood to mince words. 'Over here, Aunt Ruby,' he yelled. At least that was the intention. But owing to the amount of mud he was chewing on, it came out as 'Obberearantuby.'

The effect was immediate. She bounded over and stood over him. The end of what felt like a gun barrel was poked into his back and at the same time the beam of a torch flashed into his eyes

'I know who you are,' she said. 'You're one of Bradley's lot aren't you? A foreigner by the sound of it. Is this another of his dirty tricks? Were you hoping to frighten me by making noises and maybe shoving something nasty through the letterbox again? Lucky for me that you trod on the garden rake. That put a stop to your gallop didn't it? Anyway, you can tell your boss that he's not going to scare me. Maybe it's time I called the police.'

'Ug,' said Archie.

'And the same to you,' said Ruby. She brought the torch nearer to the scene. 'What's this?' she said, suddenly very animated. 'Do you know what you've done?' she yelled. 'You've only gone and flattened my Alpine Sunset you vandal! It's my prize winning rose and now you've ruined it!' She gave the gun another push.

'Stuffyeralpnansnst,' said Archie.

'I've had enough of this,' said his aunt. 'I know what I'll do. Wait there and don't move.' Saying which she turned and marched back into the house.

'Wait here?' Archie mused. 'Did she think he was about to rise effortlessly and take a turn round the garden with a rosebush stuck to his chest?' He moved to try and free himself and groaned as a particularly large thorn stuck itself into his leg.

When she came back she bent over him and grasped his hands. 'About time!' he thought, preparing for the heave-ho that would get him back on his feet. Instead he felt cold metal snap round his wrists.

'Regulation handcuffs,' said Ruby. 'I wasn't a policeman's wife for nothing.'

2

A few weeks earlier, two men were to be seen sitting together in the corner of a quiet country pub called the Pied Bull. They were an odd-looking couple. Charlie Leggit was a short, rounded figure of a man, dressed soberly in a suit that he managed to fill to capacity. He had the look of someone permanently pleased with himself. By contrast, his companion, a beanpole figure who looked as if he'd make a promising entry for the local scarecrow competition, was rather less sunny as he regarded his companion with a scowl.

'I don't like this,' he said.

'Why? What don't you like, Joe?'

'Well this, of course. This is the second time we've been together in public. Somebody could put two and two together and make five.'

'Relax! We're in the country, miles away from anywhere. That's why I chose it. No one we know is going to be here. Besides, we've nothing to hide. I work for an insurance company and I'm also a councillor. You run a local building business and we just happen to be friends. There's nothing wrong with that, is there?'

Joe Bradley gave him a sour look. 'Who said we were friends, councillor? You said you wanted to talk business, that's all. In future we'll meet somewhere rather less public.'

'Okay, okay!' The councillor always considered himself at his best when pouring oil on troubled waters, although some would prefer to say he was a greasy blighter. 'There's no need to get het up about it. Let's just say we have a bit of business to discuss and this is a pleasant way to do it. So let's start with the fact that you've now bought the field known around here as The Meadow, right?'

'Yeah, and made myself nearly bankrupt in the process. A field and no planning permission. What am I supposed to do with it? Grow potatoes?'

'Oh very droll Joe, but don't knock it! It's thanks to me you beat all the other bidders for that field. Anyway, the delay is due to objections from the owner of Oak Tree Cottage next door. As soon as that's sorted out, you'll be okay.'

The builder gave him a cold look. 'It's all right for you councillor, shuffling bits of paper round on your desk, but I've got a gang waiting to get started. Any more delay and I'll have to start laying some off. How come one old biddy is allowed to chuck a spanner in the works like this?'

'It's called democracy, Joe. Anyway, I thought you went to see her?'

'I did.'

'And?'

'And nothing. She refused to talk and ordered me to clear off.'

'I see. So have you tried anything else?'

'Yeah. I sent Dooley round one night with instructions to frighten her. He hung around the garden making the sorts of noises that usually scare old ladies into thinking they have a prowler. But it didn't work on her. She's tough.'

'She must be. Dooley's face is enough to scare anybody.'

Bradley looked at him scornfully. It was dark you idiot. She didn't see his face. Anyway, before he left he posted a dead rat through her letterbox.'

'And you think that scared her?'

'I dunno if it scared her or not, but now she knows who was responsible.'

'Oh, how come?'

'Because Dooley posted a card with it.'

'What sort of card?'

'A *With the compliments of builder Joe Bradley* sort of card.'

'I see. What sort of idiots do you employ, Joe?'

'The sort that'll work for half the money everyone else gets. That sort.'

'Right. Well, let me think about this.'

There was a long drawn out silence. The councillor furrowed his brow while Bradley gazed into his half-empty glass and looked despondent.

'Okay!' Leggit said finally, 'There is something else we can try.'

'Oh yeah?'

'Yeah! Suppose someone was to make an offer for the place? In the circumstances, she might think twice about turning them down. It would be an opportunity for her to end the hassle once and for all.'

The builder looked at him in disbelief. 'Oh yeah? And who d'you think would be daft enough to buy a cottage with no electricity or running water and a row hanging over it about the field next door?' he sneered.

The councillor smirked. 'Well who do you think, Joe?'

As the implication sank in, Bradley reacted furiously. 'Who, me? You can forget that idea councillor. Haven't you heard a word I've said? I'm broke!'

'Ah, but you haven't heard the best bit yet. There's no need for money to be involved. You simply offer her one of your brand new bungalows in exchange for the cottage. Tell her you'll build it to her own specification! That has to be an offer she can't refuse, right? If you could pull that off, you'd have a lot of extra land to build on, with a cottage thrown in. And you'd have no problem selling the cottage, once it was modernised!'

Bradley thought hard about the idea. He looked at it from all angles but failed to spot any immediate snags. Charlie Leggit smiled into his beer. Sometimes he dazzled himself with his own cunning.

'Okay,' said Bradley finally, 'but all this is so much hot air until I get the go-ahead to build. Just how long is it going to take?'

'You'll get the go-ahead just as soon as all the other objections have been dealt with.'

Bradley glared. 'What *other* objections? You mean there are more?'

'Joe, there are always objections to this sort of scheme. We just have to deal with them.'

'Is that so? So who are these people?'

'Well villagers, mostly. The Meadow has always been there and they'd like to keep it that way, even though it's no longer used as a kids play area. The new leisure centre takes care of all that. Anyway the point is, if our plan works and she does sell the place, that sort of opposition will fade away.'

'And what if she won't sell?'

'If she won't, then we'll just have to go back to scaring her off.'

Bradley looked incredulous. 'Oh, good. Let's try something that's already failed.'

'I've been thinking about that. It failed because it wasn't personal enough.'

'What do you mean, not personal enough?'

'Well, while a dead rat through the letterbox isn't going to scare a tough countrywoman like her, I think she'd be a lot more frightened of say, a threat to her reputation. If we could dig up something shady, we could apply a bit of pressure. After all, everyone has some sort of skeleton in the cupboard.'

'Speak for yourself. So how do we find this skeleton?'

'I'm working on it.'

'Good, well while you're planning that, you can get me another drink.'

3

'Feeling better?' Ruby enquired solicitously.

Archie was sitting by the fire with the last drops of a glass of brandy now safely inside him. He was dressed in pyjamas and a dressing gown that had belonged to Ruby's husband, Fred. While grateful for the makeshift nightwear, he couldn't help thinking that one leg of the pyjama bottoms would have made an adequate windsock for Heathrow airport.

He scowled. 'Could be worse after that ambush, I suppose.'

'Ambush? How was I to know it was you? I've already had one prowler round. You should have said something.'

'You should try holding a conversation while you're pinned to a rosebush and talking through a mouthful of mud.'

'And I'll have you know that was my favourite rose,' she said with feeling. 'It's won many a prize at the local show and I still haven't forgiven you for ruining it.'

'I'm sorry but it wasn't by choice. I felt like one of those fellas who lounge about on a bed of nails for a living.'

'I know, but it was all an accident.' She sounded hurt.

'Okay, Aunt Ruby, it wasn't your fault, but I didn't expect to find the path had moved. It used to run from the gate to the front door.'

'That was Fred's idea. He liked straight lines but I like curves so I changed it a bit. Now the path has a bend in it.'

'Well, I didn't know that of course, but what about later? Was it necessary to throw a bucket of cold water over me?'

'It was the only way to do it. There are no hosepipes here.'

'I meant why slosh water over me at all?'

'How else was I to get the mud off? I had to see who was underneath. I thought it must be the prowler again.' Ruby said unabashed. 'Anyway, none of this would have happened if you'd let me know you were coming.'

'I wanted to surprise you.'

'You did that all right. Anyway, it's so nice to see you again Archibald. You must give me all the news. Your mother does write occasionally, but it's not the same as a chat.'

Archie stifled a yawn. 'Really? Wouldn't you rather wait until morning?'

'I'm dying to hear everything now.'

'Well, there's not much to tell really,' said Archie. 'I've been staying with a friend for a couple of days and he lent me his car to get here.'

'Archibald! You know what I mean. Tell me about the family,' she commanded.

Realising she was not about to be fobbed off, he gave her a potted version of their time abroad, as best he could. 'And that's it really,' he finished. Then, in an effort not to sound too abrupt, he said, 'How about you and uncle Fred?' It was a fatal error. Ruby could be voluble on the subject of her late husband. By the time she reached the end of her narrative, Archie was drooping.

'And as you know,' she said finally, 'the end came in the garden.'

'Really?'

'Yes, I found him lying face down in a row of peas.'

14

Stifling the unworthy thought that lying down in a row of peas sounded a very attractive proposition right now, Archie said with sincerity, 'What a shock for you. I am sorry. He was a big man in every sense. Very big,' he added, plucking at the generous folds enveloping him.

'It happens,' said Ruby. 'What about you? You must be a bit tired.'

Archie stifled another yawn. 'Well now you mention it ...'

'Of course.' She went to a cupboard in the corner and produced a candle in its holder. She lit it from the fire using a taper and handed it to him. 'The bed's all ready and you know where the bedroom is.'

'I certainly do.' He pulled himself out of his chair and pecked her on the cheek.

'Goodnight Archibald.'

'Archie, please! Goodnight Aunt Ruby.'

He made his way up the old familiar staircase in one corner of the living room. At the top, he pressed down on the latch and went in. The room was exactly as he remembered it. Candlelight threw flickering shadows round the walls, recalling those halcyon days he'd spent here as a boy. He remembered setting the candle down on the floor and bouncing joyfully across the room before diving onto that huge soft feather bed. The memory was so strong, he couldn't resist a re-enactment. He put the candle down and sprang towards the bed, forgetting he was now several inches taller. At the point where the roof sloped downwards, his head came suddenly and painfully into contact with one of the old beams. He staggered around for a second or two before collapsing on the bed. As he did so, his aunt's voice came floating up. 'Remember to watch out for those low beams up there, Archibald,' she called.

4

Joe Bradley was not in the best of moods when the phone rang. 'Who is it?' he barked.

'It's me ... Charlie Leggit.'

'What do you want?'

'Are you having a bad day, Joe?'

'What makes you think I'm having any good days? What do you want?'

'Well, you remember the last time we met, I mentioned trying a more subtle approach? For instance, looking for what is generally known as "a skeleton in the cupboard".'

'What about it?'

'Well, her personal papers might give us a clue. Some old love letters, an unpaid bill or whatever. Something with a whiff of scandal about it. I'm not saying she has anything like that, but you never know. If we could take a look at her paperwork, we might find something.'

'And how do you propose to get hold of this stuff?'

'Well obviously, she wouldn't give it to us voluntarily. We'd have to take it.'

'A burglary?'

'Well, that's one way.'

'I can't think of any other way.'

'Okay, so we'd have to organise a burglary.'

'By "we" you mean me?'

'That would be good, Joe.'

'I thought so. So suppose someone did break in. How the hell would he know where to look? He'd have to ransack the place and that tends to be noisy.'

'Well, I have given the matter some thought, Joe. Suppose I arranged for an inspector to pay her a visit beforehand? He could look round and note some details of the layout and the contents? Once we had that, we could plan our next move.'

'So you have a bent inspector willing to do this have you?'

'I don't know of any bent inspectors, but I do have someone in mind. He's an actor who could play the part. A member of the local drama group.'

There was a brief silence while Bradley digested this. Eventually he said, 'Okay, I think we're grasping at straws here councillor, but I suppose anything's worth a try.'

'I'm glad we agree, Joe. We can talk more when I see you. I think we've said enough over the phone.'

'You sound nervous councillor. If I were you, I'd pour myself a drop of something strong,' said Bradley as he hung up.

5

Sidney Burke was thirty-seven years old and living with his mother. The trouble was, he'd never really grown up. Mrs Burke had hoped that by this stage she'd be able to dandle a grandchild or two on her knee but it seemed her son had other ideas.

The trouble was that Sidney was a dreamer. In his imagination, he conjured up all sorts of situations where heroic deeds were done, and he was the dashing figure at the centre. His job as a clerk working for Evesbury District Council allowed him to indulge these dreams during periods when he wasn't obliged to put in a bit of legitimate work.

At home, he read adventure stories that filled his head with tales of incredible deeds and filled the spare room with old magazines. This, in turn, filled his mother with dismay as she had envisaged the room as a guest suite for her hoped-for grandchildren. Unfortunately, all her pleas had fallen on deaf ears.

One day, he decided to join a group known as Evesbury and District Amateur Dramatics or EDAM for short. The local population considered this an appropriate title for this cheesy group but Sidney was eager to get involved. He considered he had the ability to become their leading actor who could perform heroic roles in front of appreciative audiences.

Unfortunately his abilities did not seem to impress the group as much as he'd hoped and he found himself with a series of small parts and only a few lines. Even these came to an end after he developed a habit of ad-libbing extra bits in order to boost his own part. It wasn't long before he found himself relegated to a backstage role.

Charlie Leggit, who always kept an ear to the ground, got to hear of Sidney's interests and wondered if this could be just the person he was looking for. Someone daft enough to take on the role of bogus building inspector. So, wasting no time, he called on Sidney at work to explain what he wanted.

Sidney was both flattered and delighted to have this approach from an important councillor. The fact that this was portrayed as an undercover operation intrigued him even more and he had no hesitation in agreeing to take it on. It could, he told himself, be the start of a whole new and exciting career.

Charlie Leggit, on the other hand, knew an idiot when he saw one. Now that Sidney had swallowed his story, the problem of how to gather information from Oak Tree Cottage had been solved.

If anything about this seemed fishy to Sidney, he ignored it. He was so taken by the idea of a secret assignment, that he felt no need to ask further questions and set about making plans.

Up in his bedroom at home, he looked at himself in the mirror, wondering how closely he resembled a council inspector. Not much, he had to admit as he eyed the spots. Perhaps he could cover them up with a beard. But no, that would take too long and he had orders to get on with it. Perhaps he could compromise with a moustache. Yes, he conceded, that was a possibility. Next he turned his attention to what would be the appropriate outfit. The suit and black shoes that Mrs Burke insisted he wore for work, seemed appropriate enough, though the suit was looking a bit worn. Perhaps a few extras were called for. Maybe he could wear a hat, for instance, or flourish a pipe to lend him an air of gravitas.

At that moment the phone rang. Mrs Burke answered it. 'Davina Burke speaking,' she said in her best telephone voice. 'To whom do you wish to speak?'

'Sidney, dear,' she called a moment later, 'Councillor Leggit wishes to speak with you.'

Sidney rushed eagerly down to take the call.

'We need to meet,' Leggit told him. 'Can you come to Bradley's building yard?'

Sidney felt a sudden thrill. 'What, you mean now?' he asked.

'Yes, if you can make it.'

'You do know it's dark outside?'

'Of course, but it has to be for security reasons. Do you know where to find the yard?'

'Not exactly, no.'

'Tell me where you live and I'll give you directions.'

Minutes later Sidney was on his bike, following directions. Not perhaps the mode of transport used by any of his fictional heroes, but beggars could not be choosers.

Over at the yard, Bradley was looking sceptical. 'Are you sure this fella can do it and if so, how do we know he won't go around blabbing about it?'

'Trust me Joe, he'll swallow anything we tell him as long as he thinks it's some kind of cloak and dagger operation. He's a fantasist. Well known for it. As for his ability, we're not looking for the Brain of Britain. It's straightforward enough.'

'But does he know anything about building?'

'Nothing, so far as I know, but this is one old lady we're talking about. He should be able to bluff his way past her all right.'

At that moment, Brain of Britain came in, slightly out of breath.

'Sorry to be so long,' said Sidney, but the car's out of commission just now.'

'Okay, take a seat,' said the councillor, and let me introduce Mr Joseph Bradley. He is the local builder who first brought this matter to our attention.'

Sidney held out a hand. 'Pleased to meet you, Joe. I'm Sidney Burke.'

Bradley ignored the hand. 'Yeah, they told me there was a berk on the case.'

'Right,' said Leggit hastily, 'let me just explain one or two things. This is a covert operation to try and establish certain facts and that is why we are calling on you to help.'

'Okay, but why me?'

'Well, I hear you're into acting, so this should be a piece of cake.'

Sidney again felt flattered. 'Ah, so you know about that then?' He thought it prudent not to mention that his tendency to go off script had long since barred him from appearing on stage.

'Fine,' he said. 'So what exactly is it you want me to find out?'

'Quite simple really,' said Leggit breezily. First you have to present yourself as a building inspector. That means you'll need some form of ID, can you manage that?'

'Easy!' said Sidney, confidently. I can get hold of a blank card and enter the details myself.'

'Good. You'd best not put your own name on it. Just invent something.'

'What do you suggest?'

'I'll leave that to you but I would suggest avoiding Smith or Jones. They could arouse suspicion.'

'Really? Why?'

'Because they're so common.'

'That could be a good reason for using one of them.'

'It could be, but there are plenty of other names to choose from.'

'How about Brown then?'

'I'd avoid that too. It's also rather common.'

Bradley, who had begun to show signs of impatience, suddenly exploded. 'Do you mind?" he bellowed. 'Why the hell are we arguing about names? You can call yourself Rumplebluddystil-skin for all I care. Can we just shut up and get on with it?'

'Not possible,' said Sidney.

'Eh?'

'That name. Too many letters. It would be difficult to fit it onto the space on the card,'

'Er, let's not worry about that now, Sidney,' said the councillor hastily. 'I'm sure you'll think of something suitable. Joe's right. We must move on to more important matters.'

Sidney was not at all sure that the question of names wasn't important. It was attention to that sort of detail that was the key, for example, to solving many a murder mystery. However, he didn't like the looks that the builder was giving him. 'Okay,' he said. 'So suppose I complete the ID, what comes next?'

'Well, you need to pay a call on Oak Tree Cottage in Gently village in order to gather as much information as you can. Introduce yourself to the owner, a Mrs Ruby Manning. Tell her you're there to survey the property from a security point of view and that the council want to make sure that older people are safe in their homes. Once you're in the cottage, have a look round. Get enough information to be able to make a rough sketch with the layout of the rooms and main items of furniture. Check the windows and possible alarms, though I don't think there's any electric in the place.'

Sidney thought this over. It was beginning to make him nervous. 'Er, I'm not actually a qualified surveyor you know,' he said.

'So what?' said Bradley. 'She won't know any more than you do.'

'But she might not be convinced.'

Bradley gave him a disparaging look. 'I thought you were supposed to be a good actor.'

'Yeah, but I don't write the scripts.'

'Okay, okay,' said Leggit soothingly. 'I understand your concern, Sidney, but I'm sure you could find one of the council's building handbooks and swot up a few technical terms. You can throw them into the conversation occasionally to make you sound authentic.'

'Good idea,' said Sidney, recovering some of his confidence. 'I'll do that.' He looked round. 'Is that it?'

'What do you want?' Bradley asked. 'A letter of commendation?'

'Well, it would be a help, Joe,' said Sidney.

'I'll put it in the post,' said Bradley. 'And one more thing. I'm

Mr Bradley to you, not Joe. Now clear off.'

'That's two things,' said Sidney.

6

As part of his preparation to visit to Oak Tree Cottage, Sidney still needed to complete a false identity card. He'd already purloined a blank, entered the details and now all it required was a photograph. This he planned to create by visiting the photo booth in the local department store in town. Once inside, he would use the various bits of make-up he'd pinched from the theatre to create his new persona before taking the picture. He'd abandoned the idea of cultivating his own moustache but instead would use one of the theatre's false ones. Additionally, he had a pair of horn-rimmed glasses and a large black hat.

So, first thing on Saturday morning, he was to be seen heading for the store with his bag of props. His plan was to get there early, prepare himself, take the photograph, and be away before the day's rush began.

There was no one about when he arrived at the store and he headed straight for the basement where he was able to settle himself quietly into the empty booth. It wasn't until he came to attach the moustache that he found he was short of one vital ingredient, the gum for sticking it in place. In his sudden panic, he realised the theatre would be closed at that hour and the only possible alternative would be to find a suitable substitute in the store.

Snatching up his belongings, he ran to the stairs and raced up four flights before he found an assistant. 'Glue?' she said. 'Certainly sir. It's in the household section. You can't miss it. It's in the basement, right next to the photo booth.'

By the time he got back, he was sweating freely. He found a counter with tubes of glue that, the label assured him, would stick anything to everything else. Having bought one, he raced back to the photo booth only to find it was now occupied by a couple of giggling girls. By the time they left, quite a queue had built up.

Inside the booth once more, he was determined not to be rushed. Getting the moustache stuck on in the right place was important and he made frequent checks on his appearance in the mirror.

Outside, the queue was growing impatient. Eventually the curtain was whipped back and an angry looking face pushed its way in. 'Ow much longer y'gonna be?' enquired the face.

'Sorry,' said Sidney, closing the curtain, 'I'm on important work for the council.'

The curtain opened again and the face reappeared, a bit redder this time 'Is that so? Well accordin' to my old woman, if I don't get my passport in time for the 'oliday she's booked, there won't be no cooked meals for the next month. So it's time to sling your 'ook, mate.'

Sidney stared at the intruder and weighed up his options. Any one of his comic book heroes would have stepped outside and showed this upstart who was boss. On the other hand, it was important that his face remained a match for the one in the photograph, so he couldn't risk having it rearranged.

'Just finishing,' he said as he gathered up his things and made a hurried departure.

When he arrived home, he felt irritated and peckish and wasted no time in getting to the kitchen. There Mrs Burke was busy

baking an apple pie when she suddenly found herself confronted by a stranger with glasses, a Hitler moustache and big black
hat, looking as though he'd just stepped out of a gangster film.
She let out a loud scream and fainted.

All this went through Sidney's mind as he approached Oak
Tree Cottage. He shuddered at the memory of the excoriating
remarks from Mrs Burke, when she had recovered sufficiently
to talk about men who had failed to grow up properly. What
made matters worse was when he found that the moustache was
behaving as if it was welded in place. The glue appeared to be
every bit as strong as it claimed to be and all efforts to shift it
were futile.

Although chastened by all this, Sidney's natural cockiness
never deserted him for long. So it was a determined Sidney who
walked up the path with his clipboard, to knock on the front
door of Ruby's cottage. When she appeared, he greeted her with
a flourish of his ID card and his rehearsed announcement,
'Good morning madam, William Sutton, Building Inspector,
Evesbury District Council. I take it you are Mrs Ruby Manning.'

He felt rather pleased with the name he'd given himself. She'd
be impressed. He was a bit taken aback when she seized hold of
the card and subjected it to close scrutiny.

'Yes?' she said, handing it back.

'Yes, what?'

'What is it you want?'

'Oh, er I'm a building inspector.'

'So you just said, so what do you want?'

'Oh, yes of course. I've come to inspect the er, building.'

'What for?'

'Oh, just gathering information on the state of properties in
the area.'

'Why?'

Sidney got the feeling that this wasn't going terribly well.

'Er, yes, why indeed? Well, the council want to be sure that people are er, safe in their homes. It's just a check on what facilities you have and to ensure everything is safe and secure.'

'Nice to know they care. You can tell them everything here is just fine,' said Ruby, starting to close the door.

'Er, hold on a second,' said Sidney, beginning to panic. 'I'll be in trouble if I don't take back a proper report. You don't mind answering a few questions do you?'

'You'll have to be quick. I'm in the middle of making some jam turnovers.'

'Wow, are you really?' said Sidney, his mouth beginning to water. 'Right, well perhaps we could start with the drains.'

'The drains?'

'Yes, the drains.'

'What drains?'

'Well, yours of course.'

'We do not have drains.'

'Haven't you? I mean, you must have. Everyone has. They're easy to forget of course, being out of sight and all that.'

'You'll be a long time looking,' said Ruby. We have what is known as a septic tank. We are too far away from the usual services, you see,' she explained kindly.

Sidney took a deep breath. Things didn't seem to be going quite to plan. He had spent a long time reading about drains but nowhere had there been any mention of septic tanks. He regretted having brought the subject up.

'Right, well I'm glad I cleared that one up. Perhaps we should move on to other things.' He took a surreptitious glance at his list.

'What other things?'

'Oh, er your damp course, water supply, gas and electrical connections. That sort of thing.'

'We don't have any of those things either.'

Sidney experienced a sinking feeling. 'Oh, but you must ...'

'Before you start telling me what I must have, let me tell you something about this place Mr Sutton ...'

'Who?'

'Sutton. That is your name, isn't it?'

'Is it? Oh yes, of course it is, ha, ha,' said Sidney, beginning to feel that this interview was getting out of control.'

'As I was about to say,' Ruby went on. This cottage was built in seventeen fifty-two, before any modern conveniences were thought of. We get water from a well in the yard, I cook on an open fire and the place is lit by paraffin lamps. What's more, I like it that way.'

The door started to close again.

Sidney, clutching at straws, tried a new line. 'Wow! that is impressive,' he said. 'I've always wanted to look around a building as old as this. I mean one where ordinary people used to live, and er, still do. Especially a beautiful place like this.'

'Oh?' said Ruby. She was always pleased when someone admired her cottage. 'You'd better come in then. You can look round until I've finished what I'm doing in about ten minutes time.'

Sidney awarded himself a mental pat on the back. He knew he could do it. He stepped jauntily through the door and past the little woman he now felt would be putty in his hands.

'Don't move another step until you've taken your hat off and wiped your feet,' said Ruby.

7

Archie arrived back at the cottage after a morning spent fishing. At least that was his excuse. He was not really interested in the sport, but it was a great autumn day and he did enjoy being outdoors, especially down by the river. He knew his uncle Fred's old fishing gear was still in the shed and that gave him the perfect excuse for lounging about on the riverbank. So he spent the next couple of hours sitting on a canvas stool, his back against a tree, holding the rod and watching the water ripple by. The fish at that point were probably quite pleased to see him. They knew a dud fisherman when they saw one.

As he put the gear back in the shed and stepped into the garden, he saw Sidney who was just leaving. Archie watched him swagger down to the gate before going indoors to find Ruby in the kitchen.

'That,' she said in answer to his question, 'was Inspector Sutton, according to the card he showed me, anyway.'

'Really? What do the police want?'

'Not the police. He was a building inspector, or so he said. He seemed very interested in drains.'

'Really? Oh well, it takes all sorts. Did you enlighten him?'

'Oh I enlightened him all right. He now knows we don't have any. Anyway, he came in, had a look round and then left thanking me profusely. But I am a bit worried about one thing though.'

'What's that then?'

'I don't think I've put enough jam in these jam turnovers.'

'Please,' said Archie, 'don't spare the jam on my account. So what was this inspection all about?'

'He gave me some cock and bull story about the council being concerned with resident safety. I didn't take much notice.'

'What made you think it was a cock and bull story?'

'Because he was a phoney. Pass the jam please, Archibald.'

'Really?' said Archie, passing the requisite item. 'And how did you come to that conclusion, Miss Marple?'

'Well first, he knew as much about buildings as I know about Croatian country dancing. Then he seemed to forget his own name, probably because he'd just invented it. And third, there was his appearance. Big floppy hat and a moustache that was stuck on. Apart from the fact that it didn't match his hair, he'd stuck it on at a bit of an angle. He looked as if he'd just stepped out of a bad play.'

'Okay, so why did you let him into the cottage?'

'Just curiosity I suppose. I wanted to see what he was up to. Also, he said the cottage was beautiful and he'd like to see more.'

'Ah, I see! Flattery got him in, did it? What did you say his name was?'

'Sutton. William Sutton it said on his card.'

Archie frowned in concentration. 'I'm sure I've heard that name somewhere before. Perhaps it'll come to me later. So, did you decide what it was all about?'

'Not really. Er, excuse me while I get these in the oven. I'm still wondering.'

'Well what did he actually do after he got in?'

'He wandered around and made notes on a clip board.'

'And did you ask him what the notes were about?'

'I did and he was very vague. Just collecting information,' he said. 'He'd already given me some guff about the council's anxiety over residents' safety.'

'A likely story ... ah, a nice cup of tea, thank you Aunt!' They were both silent while they sipped and pondered.

'Why,' said Archie eventually, 'would anyone, even an idiot such as the one we seem to have here, suddenly take it into his head to pose as a council inspector?'

'Somebody put him up to it?'

'A shrewd observation.'

'Now who's dishing out the flattery? Have you just had a whiff of my baking, Archibald?'

'There's no getting past you is there?'

'Well it's not ready yet ... So, who could be behind it?'

'I don't know. We'll just have to wait and see. In the meantime, don't let any more strange men wander round the place.'

'I wouldn't normally but as I said before, I was curious.'

'Well, you know what curiosity did, don't you? ... Here! hang on a minute. I've just remembered where that name came from ... William Sutton ... he was an American bank robber!'

'Why would he choose to call himself after an American bank robber?'

'I don't know but my guess is that this fellow is some sort of fantasist. He imagines himself as a hero and wants to copy someone he admires. Sutton was a master of disguise, so perhaps this bogus inspector saw him as a sort of role model.'

'Some model,' sniffed Ruby. 'All I can say is that I've never heard of this William Sutton.'

'I don't suppose you have. When it comes to robbing banks, he's not nearly as famous as Bonnie and Clyde for instance. All the same, Willy Sutton was a pretty cool character.'

'How come you remember him?'

'Well, he seems to have been quite a witty sort. Most famously, when he was asked why he robbed banks, he reportedly said,

"Because that's where the money is". Quite witty, don't you think?'

Ruby sniffed again. 'That's all we need, witty criminals.'

'Okay,' said Archie, 'subject closed. So tell me about this builder. Where did he spring from?'

'Ah, Joe Bradley! I don't know that much about him. I knew his father better. He was a good builder, old Sam Bradley. He founded the business and made a good thing out of it because he was trusted. You can't say the same about his son. He's a dodgy type even if he did go to university.'

'Joe Bradley went to university?'

'And private school before that. Sam wanted his son to have the education he never had. The business was prospering, so he could afford it.'

'So what happened to the father? Retired did he?'

'Sadly not. He had a heart attack and died a couple of years ago. Joe took over the business and was able to trade on his father's good name for a while, but it's all gone downhill since. He's been involved in too many shady deals.'

'I see. Not just a bad 'un but an educated bad 'un. The worst kind. We'd better keep an eye on him.'

Ruby pulled a face. 'Perhaps, but he's not going to lose me any sleep.'

8

Sidney and Charlie Leggit sat in Bradley's office waiting for him to appear. The builder, apparently, was busy taking delivery of a load of second-hand radiators that he was intending to have painted and installed in one of his 'modernised' old properties.

Sidney was feeling rather pleased with himself in spite of being unable to rid himself of the false moustache. Leggit, on the other hand, was wondering if he'd made a mistake in getting a half-wit like Sidney, involved. Sidney was not answering any questions until he had a full audience.

When Joe Bradley finally came in, he looked none too pleased. 'Those radiators are rubbish,' he complained. 'They're only fit for the scrap heap.'

'So you'll have to write them off then?' said Leggit.

'Not if I can help it. They'll have to do. I can't afford to lose money on them.'

'Well, as you can see Joe, Sidney is with us and he has, I hope, got something to cheer you up.'

'Oh, yeah?'

'Yes,' said Sidney, 'The visit to the cottage was a great success.' He paused for applause but it was apparent his audience had not yet warmed up.

'Well, go on then,' said Leggit.

'Yes, well I got what you asked for. Mind you, it wasn't easy. But my experience in the theatre stood me in good stead. I used a disguise and a false ID to get into the cottage. It was rather brilliant actually.'

Bradley gave him a sour look. 'I did wonder about that fungus under your nose,' he said. 'So you got in, but did you get me what I wanted?'

'Of course,' said Sidney, a trifle miffed. 'Anyway, I've made a sketch as you asked,' he said, taking a piece of folded paper from his pocket and handing it over with a flourish, 'I think I did rather well, considering she was watching me the whole time.'

Bradley unfolded the paper and spent a moment studying it.

'Okay,' he said finally, that's it. You can go now.'

Sidney was taken aback. This was his moment of glory and he thought it deserved a better reception than it was currently getting. 'Don't you want to hear more? There's a lot more to tell.'

'You can tell it to the councillor. I've got all I need, so I suggest you shove off.'

'I say ...' Sidney started.

'It's all right Sidney,' said Councillor Leggit soothingly. 'You can go and I'll see you later.'

Reluctantly, Sidney rose, tugged angrily at his moustache and walked off. He cast a final dirty look in Bradley's direction before the door closed behind him.

'A pain in the ear, that one,' said Bradley.

'Oh, but he has his uses Joe, and he did do what you wanted,' said the councillor soothingly. He seems to have provided a good sketch.'

'Okay, but we don't need him now. What we do need is to plan this break-in. I hope it's going to be worth it.'

'I'm hopeful there'll be something we can use.'

'You think we might?'

'We won't know until we've looked, will we? According to Sidney's information, there's an old cabin trunk and a dresser in the living room. We could find something interesting there.'

'Yeah, maybe.'

'Well, it's a long shot of course. Are you sure you've got some-body who can do the job?'

'Of course I have, provided there's an entry point.'

'And is there?'

'I've made sure there is. According to Dooley she leaves the small kitchen window open at night.'

'But how does anyone get through a small window?'

Bradley gave him a sour look. 'You know, councillor, you ask far too many questions. Just leave it with me, all right?'

'Of course, Joe. But is this burglar fellow discreet?'

'Oh, he's discreet all right. He knows he has to be. Anyway, this was all your idea so I hope for your sake it's not a waste of everybody's time.'

Charlie Leggit thought about this. Well, we've nothing to lose, Joe. If we find what I hope we'll find, we'll be on a winner.'

9

Archie sat up in bed wondering why he was suddenly awake. Usually he slept like the proverbial log. He consulted his watch with the aid of a torch and saw that it was just after three fifteen. It was very tempting to lie back and doze off again but he knew he should investigate. Slipping out of bed, he made his way gingerly to the door and eased it open. The trouble with this old place was that everything seemed to creak and groan as soon as you touched it. He eased open the door and peered out into the blackness, listening for anything unusual. There wasn't a sound to be heard and he was wondering whether it was all just imagination when there was a brief flash of light from the direction of the kitchen.

It could, of course, be his Aunt Ruby, but he knew that was unlikely. She was an even sounder sleeper than he was and slept with her head under the blanket to make sure it stayed that way. He knew it was time to investigate.

Hanging behind the door was an old dressing gown. Slipping it on, he eased his way onto the stairs and made his way down, avoiding the now familiar creaky bits. At the bottom he paused before taking a few careful steps to his left to in order to miss the big old table and chairs that occupied the middle of the room. This left the way clear for a quick dash to the kitchen, with all the advantages of speed and surprise.

Taking a deep breath, Archie launched himself forwards at speed. The surprise came a moment later when the hastily-tied dressing gown cord came undone, and he stood on the loose end. Head down, he charged forward through the kitchen door and straight into Ruby's collection of pots and pans. The noise was horrendous. The next second, the intruder had flung the door open and fled.

A dazed Archie muttered a curse as he picked himself up and set off unsteadily in pursuit. As he crossed the rough concrete of the yard, he immediately regretted the absence of footwear and it was a relief when he left the hard surface for the relative softness of the lawn. This, however, was short lived when the soles of his feet were suddenly subjected to sharp stabbing pains. His immediate thought was that the intruder was cunningly scattering tin tacks in his wake causing him to leap about, uttering a few well known phrases.

At that moment a bright light shone upon the scene and behind it was Ruby, whose defences against being disturbed had been penetrated by the racket in the kitchen. She was carrying the shotgun. 'Freeze!' she bawled.

'I wish I could,' panted Archie, still making known his opinion of gardens that were full of mantraps with needle sharp points.

She shone the torch on him. 'Archibald!' what are you doing out here at this time of night, jumping around under the holly tree. Is this some sort of ritual dance?'

'Nothing of the kind. I was chasing a burglar,' he said, hopping out of the danger zone to collapse on the grass.

'A burglar? Don't be silly. I've got nothing worth burgling.'

'Apparently he didn't know that.'

'And just look at your poor feet,' she said, as she watched him pull out the bits of holly still embedded in his extremities. 'Why didn't you put some shoes on?'

'I was in a bit of a hurry at the time.'

'And was there any need for all that language?' she asked primly. 'I shall have to get the swear box out again. It hasn't been used since Fred departed,' she sighed.

'Okay,' said Archie, thinking it best to move on. 'So you don't think you've anything worth pinching. Are you sure? What about jewellery for instance?'

'I was never really one for jewellery. The only things I've got are the wedding ring on my finger and a necklace that Fred bought for our anniversary. Certainly nothing worth burgling the place for.'

'I see. Well perhaps we should get back to bed and talk about it in the morning.'

'That's a very good idea, Archibald.'

'I'm full of them,' said Archie. 'Goodnight, Aunt Ruby.'

Next morning, Archie pushed away from the table feeling ready for the day ahead. A full plate of eggs and bacon was always a good start for him but he was also feeling a little guilty about not doing more for his aunt. It was time to start helping in earnest.

'It's time I started pulling my weight around here,' he told his aunt, as she bustled in to clear the table.

'What are you talking about?'

'Well here I am, enjoying the benefits of your hospitality and doing very little in return. I must find out more about this house building business. I'll start talking to the locals today and get some opinions.'

She nodded. 'Maybe that's not such a bad idea. You could have a word with Bradley's foreman for instance.'

He looked astonished. 'Bradley's foreman? You want me to talk to the enemy?'

'He's not the enemy. He was old Sam's foreman and just as honest. He carried on in the job of foreman when Joe took over but he doesn't think much of Joe's methods. He knows more about the business than anyone, so Joe can't afford to lose him. Anyway, it's just a thought.'

'And a very good one. I'll try to run into this character, I think.'

'Well his name is Al Richards. You might find him in The Blue Barrel in Evesbury.'

'Wow, you're a mine of information Aunt. I don't know where you get it from.'

'Your Uncle Fred, of course. He knew everybody round the town as well as this village. That's why he was so good at his job.'

'The more I learn about him the more I'm amazed. It's okay Aunt Ruby, you sit down and I'll wash up this morning.'

She made a beeline for the table and started collecting plates. 'There's really no need. I'll wash and you can wipe if you like. That way we can talk about last night.'

As they got busy in the kitchen, Archie said, 'I'd like to know what our visitor was after. Was he just trying his luck or was he after something in particular?'

'Did you actually see him?' Ruby asked.

'Yes, I did. There was a misty sort of moon and I caught a glimpse of him hot-footing it across the garden.'

'Could you describe him?'

'A sort of shadowy grey figure moving at speed.'

'Not much to go on, is it?'

'I'm afraid not.'

They fell silent again.

'One thing I don't understand,' said Ruby, suddenly. 'We both sleep well. It's a family trait. I only woke up because it sounded like the roof was falling in. But what about you?'

'Good question,' said Archie. 'When I woke up it was all very quiet, but there must have been a noise or something to disturb me. But how do you know what it was, if you were asleep at the time?'

'We need to think,' said Ruby. 'What could he have been up to?'

'Looking for something obviously, but exactly what? I know he had a torch because I saw a flash of light. Anyway, let's take a look round the scene of the crime. We'll finish up here and start a search.'

When they were ready, they went into the living room. Ruby went over to the old dresser in the corner. She opened and closed each of the drawers in turn, checking the contents. 'Hear that?' she said.

'Hear what?'

'Exactly! The drawers glide in and out without a sound. Do you know,' she said as if addressing a group of visitors in a stately home, 'this piece is over a hundred and seventy years old!'

'Really. They don't make them like that these days.'

'They do not.'

'Ditto with this trunk,' said Archie, demonstrating the noiselessness by opening and closing the lid. He took a peek inside. 'Bit of a waste of good space, isn't it?'

'What do you mean?'

'I mean you could use it for storage purposes.'

'I do use it for storage purposes. I keep my papers in it.'

'Do you? Well there's nothing in here at the moment.'

'Of course there is. There should be a couple of birth certificates, a few letters, some bills, that sort of stuff. I do have a clear-out from time to time and burn the unwanted on the bonfire in the garden.'

'I can assure you Aunt Ruby, there's nothing in here at the moment. Come and see for yourself.'

She hurried over and peered into the trunk. 'We've been robbed!'

'Looks like it.'

'So that explains the break-in.'

'But what would anyone want with my old bills and things?'

'Are you sure there was nothing of importance?'

'Nothing much. There were some birth certificates, but they can be replaced.'

'Very strange. Mind you, they wouldn't stop to sort it out. They'd just grab the lot so they could sort through it later.'

'But what could they possibly want?'

'That,' said Archie, 'will have to remain a mystery for the moment. But at least I now realise what woke me up.'

'What?"

'He must have accidentally done this,' said Archie, letting the lid fall with a bang.

10

The more Archie thought about the removal of documents, the less sense it made. 'I suppose it will all become clear in the course of time,' he said as his aunt bustled about, attending to all the things she considered needed attention in the well-run home.

'I hope so ... coffee?' she asked.

'Thank you, Aunt Ruby. I think I'll pay a visit to that pub you mentioned, to see if Bradley's foreman is there.'

'Of course ... Al Richards ... I know he used to lunch in The Blue Barrel, so maybe you'll be lucky.'

'Okay. I'll pay them a visit. Between twelve and one o'clock, do you think?'

'Probably about right. Unless he's changed his habits lately.'

'Okay, I'll take the car.'

'Will it get you that far?'

'Fingers crossed. Oh, by the way, it's mine now.'

'What's yours?'

'The car of course. Yesterday, I phoned Doug, that's the friend who lent it me, and he told me I could keep it.'

'What, the car?'

'Yes, the car.'

'That was very generous of him.'

'Well yes, except that it's going to cost more in repairs than it's actually worth.'

'I see. A fool's bargain you mean?'

'Thank you. I thought you might see it that way.'

'Well, don't come to me with the repair bill.'

'Of course not. Anyway, if it conks, I can always walk.'

'Are you up to walking a couple of miles? How are your poor feet after last night?'

'Never better,' said Archie. 'That acupuncture is a wonderful thing.'

The Blue Barrel was crowded with customers at various stages of eating and drinking as Archie pushed his way to the bar. 'Excuse me, I'm looking for Al Richards,' he said to the barman who was busy pouring a pint.

'Yes, mate. Usual place, over there,' the barman replied, waving a hand towards a table near the window,

Archie saw a rugged looking, grey haired chap, apparently in the last stages of demolishing a ploughman's lunch.

'Thanks,' he said to the barman. 'A pint of your best bitter and an orange juice please, when you're ready.'

He was carrying the drinks over when he saw the builder stand up, ready to leave. The man grinned as he approached. 'Well spotted,' he said. 'It's not always easy to find a table at this time.'

'Thanks,' said Archie, setting the drinks down, 'but I was hoping to have a word.'

The smile faded from the builder's face. 'I'm sorry,' he said. 'If it's a complaint then you'll have to contact Mr Bradley. He's the boss.' He took a step towards the door.

'It's not a complaint, I just wanted to talk. You're Al Richards aren't you?' He held out a hand. 'My name is Archie Graham and I'm the nephew of Ruby Manning, widow of the late Sergeant Fred Manning, and my uncle-in-law. Perhaps you remember him?'

The builder's frosty manner suddenly melted away. 'Fred Manning! Of course I remember old Fred. The best copper we ever had round here.' He took Archie's hand and shook it warmly. 'I should be getting back but a few more minutes won't hurt. What can I do for you?'

As they both sat down, Archie said, 'the fact of the matter is that my aunt is being harassed by your boss in various ways and I want to do something about it. He's trying to get her to drop her opposition to this housing scheme of his on The Meadow.'

'Oh that! Can't help you there I'm afraid as I'm not directly involved at the moment. He's got me doing up some old houses for resale. I've already told him the people round here don't want his housing scheme and would rather The Meadow was left as it is. But he doesn't pay much attention to anything I say. Not about the way the business is run, anyway.'

'I see. But if so many are against it, surely he doesn't stand much chance of getting planning consent.'

'Oh, I'm not saying that.' He looked round and lowered his voice. 'You see he has contacts on the local council.'

'Go on,' said Archie encouragingly.

'I think I've probably said enough already. Let's just say you should take a good look at the way the planning committee is run.'

'Say no more, that confirms my suspicions.' Archie indicated the pint glass. 'Now, would you like another drink, Al?'

'Thanks all the same, but I'd better get on with that bathroom I'm installing. It's proving a bit tricky with all the old plumbing. In fact, I'm having to rip most of it out.'

'That sounds expensive.'

'You're right. The boss would have made do with the old stuff, but he does things his way and I do them mine.'

'Good to hear. Are you sure you couldn't manage another?'

'Better not,' said Al, 'I need to keep a clear head for that bathroom. I can't leave it half-finished and without hot water.'

'You never spoke a truer word,' said Archie, feelingly. 'It's barbaric to be without it, especially in weather like this.'

There was a moment's silence while they contemplated life without hot water.

'Well,' said Archie eventually, 'I won't drink all of this because

I'm driving, but why don't we have a half each?'

'Go on then.'

'Good,' said Archie, as he poured a half into the builder's empty glass. 'That just leaves the orange.'

'Don't look at me. I hate the stuff.'

'Okay, maybe the pot plant in the window would like it.'

'It does look a bit dry.'

'Say no more,' said Archie, picking up the glass and tipping the contents into the nearby pot. 'It looks like an aspidistra. My aunt's got one in her window.'

'Does it like orange?'

'Not to my knowledge, but I'm sure it will appreciate the change.'

'Let's hope so.' Al raised his glass. 'Cheers, anyway.'

'Cheers,' said Archie, 'and good luck with the plumbing.'

After they'd touched glasses and drunk, Archie said, 'I believe you used to work for Bradley senior. My aunt says Sam Bradley was not only a good builder, but reliable and honest with it.'

'Well, she's right there. Those were the days when I enjoyed the work. It's not the same now and to be honest, I can't wait to retire.'

'Really? Have you much longer to go?'

'Eleven months, providing he doesn't sack me before.'

'Is that likely?'

'I don't think so. I'm sure he'd like to but I'm equally sure he won't. He knows that I know too much about his business. I can't see him risking a disgruntled ex-employee, blowing the gaff on him.'

'I see. So what happens when you do retire? Will you look for another job?'

'I don't think so. I've had enough of the building business

under people like him. No, the first priority will be to get my own house sorted. The wife says I spend all my time perfecting other people's properties but haven't decorated a single room at home for the last ten years. She's right and she deserves better. Besides, I won't have any pressing financial problems. The house is ours and thanks to old Sam, I invested in a good pension scheme, so I can leave at any time without worry.'

'Well, I hope it goes well. I'll bet if my uncle was here he'd say the same thing.'

'I'm sure you're right. Old Fred was one of the best.'

They were silent again, remembering the man who served the community without fear or favour.

'Well,' said Al, draining his glass, 'I must be off. Good luck with the battle to come. I can't wait to see the boss's face if he loses this one.'

'You and a lot of others, Al. And thanks for all the help. By the way, is there anyone in particular I should look out for on that planning committee?'

'Well a lot of them are getting on a bit. Chosen, apparently because of their "experience." I'm told by someone who was once on the committee, that they are about as dynamic as cold rice pudding. They meet, drink tea, talk about things that don't concern them and leave most of the decision-making to the chairman.'

'Charlie Leggit,' said Archie, 'that much I do know.'

'Then maybe you should talk to him,' said Al, draining his glass in one big swallow. 'Well, I really must be going.' He held out his hand. 'Thanks for the drink. Nice meeting you, Archie.'

'You too Al.'

As he turned to go, Al hesitated. 'Oh, by the way, I don't know how significant this is, but for the last few weeks, Joe Bradley has been mysteriously disappearing for part of the weekend. Running a business is a seven day affair and something often crops up out of normal hours. But it seems that no one has been able to contact our Joe on a Saturday evening or during Sunday. Nobody knows what he gets up to, but he's obviously got something going. Anyway, I just thought I'd mention it.'

'I'm glad you did. It gives me something else to ponder on. Thanks Al.'

'Okay, I'll be off then.'

Archie watched the departing figure disappearing through the door.

'Thanks Al,' he muttered, 'this thing gets murkier by the minute.'

11

'Was the trip worthwhile?' Ruby asked, as Archie came in to the living room, fresh from his ablutions.

'I think so,' he said, as he sat in front of the fire. 'I tell you what would be good though.'

'Go on. Surprise me.'

'I was thinking how nice it would be to have hot water in the house.'

'We've got hot water in the house. I just boiled two kettles full for you.'

'Yes, and that was very kind of you but I was thinking more along the lines of it being on tap.'

'What?' she said indignantly. 'Do you mind? It would cost a fortune to install a hot water system in this old place. You should be here when there's a hard frost. Then you're lucky if ...'

'Okay, okay,' said Archie, hastily raising his hand. 'It was just a thought. In answer to your question ... yes it was worth the trip. I saw Al Richards and ...'

'And once you have a hot water system Archibald, you use more water. And as our only water supply is ...'

'From the well. Yes, yes I know, Aunt Ruby. I'm sorry, I wasn't thinking. Can we get back to Al Richards?'

'Did he mention hot water systems?'

'No, but he did give a strong hint about the local planning committee. I got the impression we should keep a close eye on them. Particularly the chairman.'

'Isn't he called Leggit.?'

'He is,' said Archie, pleased he'd got the subject back on track. 'And apparently, a very powerful influence.'

'So he's the one doing all the pushing for this housing scheme?'

'Looks like it.'

Ruby looked thoughtful. 'I think I'll have to have a word with Lucy Gemmel this afternoon. I'll see her at The Ladies Club.'

'Who is Lucy Gemmel and what is The Ladies Club?'

'Lucy Gemmel is a friend who happens to work for the council. She may be able to tell me something about this Leggitt. As for The Ladies Club, it is a club for ladies, and I am one of them.'

'Thanks for clarifying that. So this Lucy knows all the gossip does she?'

'*Information*, not gossip, Archibald. I'll find out what she knows. Anyway, I'd like you to come along too. You can talk to Lucy about hot water systems. She's just had a new boiler put in. She said it was a nightmare!'

'Okay, okay, you win. I won't mention hot water systems ever again. Just tell her that I'm quite happy with what we've got.'

'And to make things worse, she had a dental appointment on the same day.'

'Was she having much done?'

'Yes, she had quite a few teeth out.'

'Good grief! Teeth out and a boiler in on the same day ... She has had it rough!'

Ruby's expression remained stern but her mouth twitched a little at the corners. 'Right, Archibald,' she said, 'The Ladies Club meeting is at two o'clock in the village hall. It isn't that far but I was wondering if you could give me a lift?'

'It would be my pleasure!' said Archie.

As they came to a noisy halt outside Gently village hall, a buzz of conversation floated out through the open door. Ruby climbed out and waved a hand towards a couple of parked cars. 'You can park over there if you like. It'll be quite safe.'

'I know it will,' said Archie, 'no one's going to pinch this old wreck. Anyway, I was thinking I might come back later to pick you up.'

'You can't do that,' said Ruby. 'They're dying to meet you. Come on inside and I'll introduce you to everybody. You must have met some of them the last time you were here. Don't worry,' she added, 'there are quite a few young ones amongst them now.'

'That's what I thought. What sort of numbers are we talking here?'

'Well it varies, but usually about thirty or so.'

'Thirty! That's an awful lot of introductions.'

'What's the matter, don't you like women?'

'Well of course I like women but they can be a bit intimidating *en masse*.'

'A bit shy eh? They'll like that.'

'Not if I don't meet them, they won't.'

'Archibald, please! They are expecting you. You don't want to let me down, do you?'

'Expecting me? How come they know I'm here?'

'Word soon gets around.'

'So it seems ... all right, I'll come in on one condition.'

'Oh, what's that?'

'That you introduce me as Archie and not Archibald.'

'But I like Archibald!'

'And I much prefer Archie.'

'Oh, all right, if you're going to be stubborn about it. Now, I'll wait while you park the wreck.'

Inside the hall, the ladies stood chattering in groups. Archie followed his aunt inside and was alarmed to notice that the sound level suddenly dropped as they all turned to stare.

Ruby made her way towards a large lady in a big hat. 'Mildred!' she said. 'May I introduce you to my nephew, er, Archie. This is Mrs Crouch, the vicar's wife, Archie.'

'How do you do?' said Archie politely.

'Delighted to meet you Archibald,' said the vicar's wife, seizing his hand and pumping it enthusiastically. 'I've heard so much about you.'

'You have?' said Archie, retrieving his hand and surreptitiously checking his fingers. 'I was just saying to my aunt that I really shouldn't be, er, intruding on a ladies' meeting.'

'Intruding? Nonsense, you are more than welcome. We often have men here. In fact our local MP, George Winder, is coming to talk to us today about "Democracy in Action." It should be fascinating and I'm sure we're all looking forward to it, isn't that so, Ruby?'

'Of course, Mildred,' said Ruby, with a slightly glazed look in her eye. She was not a fan of politicians but sometimes it was as well to keep your thoughts to yourself.

'And now you really must excuse me,' said Mrs Crouch briskly. I have a few things to do, then we must get started.' With that, she bustled away.

Ruby took Archie by the elbow and steered him round the room, introducing him to various ladies, some young and some not so young, while he did his best not to look like a rabbit caught in the headlights.

He was thankful when the voice of Mrs Crouch was heard from the front of the hall. 'Ladies! Please be seated,' she boomed.

There ensued a period of shuffling and scraping as they settled down into the rows of chairs.

'Before we begin,' Mrs Crouch went on, 'could I just offer on behalf of us all, a very warm welcome to Ruby's nephew, Archibald, who is back in this country for the first time in many years.'

There was a sudden, spontaneous burst of applause and someone gave a loud whistle. At the same time he felt a sharp dig in the ribs from his aunt. 'Stand up!' she hissed.

Archie, feeling like a memorial plaque that had just been unveiled, stood up, grinned and nodded vaguely around before he sat down again.

'Excellent!' Mrs Crouch was getting into her stride. 'Today ladies, we will be honoured with a visit from our MP, Mr George Winder, in,' glancing at her watch, 'about half an hour's time. In the meantime we could decide on some questions to ask him.'

Ruby was quickest off the mark. 'I have something that I think is important to the village,' she said.

'Yes, Ruby dear?'

Ruby stood up and looked calmly round the sea of expectant

faces. 'It's about The Meadow,' she said. 'As we all know, it is a beautiful grassy area by the river that's been there forever and has been used by villagers and visitors alike. It's a place for adults to enjoy and rest, while children can run around there, freely and safely.' She paused dramatically. 'And now, almost unnoticed, it's been sold off to a builder who proposes to build houses on it. Of course, this isn't news to you ladies, but I feel we should start to get much more active in stopping this vandalism before it's too late!'

With that, she sat down.

'Brilliant!' Archie murmured as the room burst into spontaneous applause.

'I agree with Mrs Manning,' piped up a voice. It was one of the younger members. 'We've tended to accept it because we think the council knows best, but maybe they don't. Maybe we ought to do something before we lose a safe place, particularly for the kids.'

There were more shouts of 'hear, hear!' from around the hall.

'Just hold on a moment!' It was a woman of nondescript appearance but with a rather fierce eye. She was, Ruby explained later, Annie Hornby, otherwise known as Awkward Annie. The title had been awarded, it was further explained, because of Annie's tendency to oppose everyone else's views. This apparently was based on her belief that she was the only one who knew what she was talking about.

'Yes, Annie?' said Mrs Crouch, keeping to her strictly neutral attitude.

'It's all very well talking about lovely landscapes and all that, but people need houses. My daughter's gettin' married soon and she needs somewhere to live that she can afford. So why not on The Meadow which is lyin' idle for most of the time.'

'Just like my 'usband,' said a voice.

This seemed to go down well with the crowd.

'There seems to be a rather raucous element in today,' said Mrs Crouch in an aside. Aloud, she said, 'Yes, well you do have a point, Annie. Anyone else?'

'I agree with Annie,' said Ruby. We do need more houses.'

'Here, steady on,' muttered Archie.

'The question is, where should they go?'

There was silence.

'I have a suggestion,' Ruby went on. Why not build them on the site of the old cheese factory?'

There was more silence as this was digested.

'That's a very good idea!' someone said. There were murmurs of approval all round.

'It won't work!' Awkward Annie was back in the fray. The land would have to be cleared first and that costs money. Builders don't like it.'

Suddenly Archie stood up. 'Excuse me ladies,' he said. 'I know this debate is none of my business, but would you mind if I offered an opinion?'

'Oh, please do, Archibald!' Mrs Crouch beamed.

'Houses built on the factory site may cost a little more, but wouldn't that be a price worth paying? Not only would we be preserving The Meadow, the most attractive spot in the village but also removing a building that is little more than an eyesore. So I propose we follow my aunt's suggestion. What do you say?'

'Absolutely,' said a voice. 'Let's tell the council to cheese it!'

This caused a sudden outburst of applause as the ladies clapped, stamped their feet and cheered, shaking the foundations and bringing dust down from the roof beams.

'I MUST SAY,' said a voice, shouting above the noise, 'IT'S

VERY KIND OF YOU TO WELCOME ME IN THIS WAY!'

Mrs Crouch beamed at the portly chap who'd just entered the room.

'*Mister* Winder!' she said, 'How nice to see you!'

12

'Well?' said Bradley, 'What did you make of it?'

The 'it' was in a pile in front of them. It consisted of papers extracted from Ruby's cottage during the recent burglary.

'Not much, to be honest,' said the councillor. 'It's a mixture of bills, receipts and personal stuff like letters, invitations, certificates and so on.'

'Did you read it all?'

'Well of course I read it all. But there was nothing significant. Not unless you're interested in the fact that she won the Gently Annual Cake Making Competition for four years in a row?'

'No, I'm not. What about the bills. Any big ones?'

'The biggest one was for her husband's funeral. Otherwise, just small ones.'

'All paid?'

'Yes, all paid. She doesn't appear to owe anybody anything.'

'What about the legal stuff regarding the cottage. Deeds and so on?'

'There's none. They're probably deposited with her solicitor.'

Bradley scowled. 'So much for your bright idea, councillor. Just a waste of time.'

'Perhaps not perhaps entirely, Joe. What's interesting is what *isn't* there.'

'What isn't there? What's that supposed to mean?'

'Well, I found copies of birth certificates for her and her husband but no marriage certificate.'

'What's a marriage certificate got to do with anything?'

'Well, don't you see?' said Leggit, smugly, 'if there's no marriage certificate, then maybe she and Fred Manning weren't actually married! In this community, she is seen as a model of propriety. A lady with old fashioned values. If it was realised that she was living with this man but not married to him, her reputation would suffer. That's something she would definitely not want. We need more information of course, to check the facts, so I've got Sidney Burke doing some research at the Registry Office.'

Bradley chewed this over. 'I suppose it could work,' he said eventually. 'From what I've heard, she does seem a bit old school. So when can we expect to hear from this berk?'

'I asked Sidney to come here this morning.'

'When?'

'He should be here by now.'

At that moment, there was a knock on the door of Bradley's hut. It was a timid sort of knock as if Sidney's usual bumptious approach had been toned down by the memory of his last hasty exit when he'd been virtually chucked out.

'That'll be him now.'

'Well don't just sit there.'

Councillor Leggit heaved himself up and went to open the door. 'Come in Sidney,' he said as Sidney stepped forward and fell over the weatherboard at the bottom of the opening. 'And make yourself comfortable,' he added as Sidney picked himself up.

Sidney, who often dreamed of himself as one of his storybook heroes, thought it was time he asserted himself. Not perhaps just now but as soon as he'd properly worked out how to get his revenge. In the meantime he thought it best to appear friendly. 'Er, good afternoon,' he said.

'Well?' said Bradley.

'Very well, thank you,' said Sidney,

'That's good,' said the councillor before Bradley could speak. 'So how did you get on with your enquiries?'

'Well, it wasn't easy ...' Sidney began.

'Are they or aren't they?' said Bradley.

'Are they or aren't they what?'

'Sidney,' said the councillor hastily, 'all we want is to know whether or not there is evidence to show that Fred Manning and Ruby were married.'

'Not,' said Sidney.

'Not what?'

'Not evidence to show they were married.'

'Let's get this clear. So there is no evidence that Ruby and Fred Manning were ever married?'

'Yes.'

'Yes, as in yes there is no evidence?'

'Yes.'

'So according to the evidence, or lack of it, they weren't married?'

'No.'

'Don't you mean yes?'

'No.'

'For God's sake,' Bradley exploded, 'is there a certificate or not?'

'No.'

'So they were never married?'

'Yes.'

'Don't you mean no?'

'No, I meant yes, they were never married.'

'Should I put the kettle on?' said Councillor Leggit.

13

Ruby was busy in the kitchen when Councillor Leggit called. Archie was out so she was cautious in opening the door.

'Yes?' she said

'Good afternoon madam, may I introduce myself? I'm Charles Leggit of Evesbury and District Council. May I have a word?'

'About what?'

'Well, about anything really. Do you think we could talk indoors?'

'You can say what you have to say here.'

Leggit felt disappointed. He had hoped to be sitting down with a cup of tea and a slice of prize winning cake.

'Well, yes, fine. Er, according to our council records, this place is owned by a Mrs Ruby Manning. I take it that is you?'

'Take it how you like. I am Ruby Manning.'

'Ah, excellent! Being on the council it's easy to lose touch with the people you represent so I am trying to make up for that by meeting as many as possible.'

'Good for you. Now if you don't mind, I am rather busy.' The door started to close.

'Please don't be too hasty. You might be interested to hear that we are about to publish a quarterly leaflet called "Council News" which will be delivered free of charge through your door, starting in two weeks. As a resident, would you be interested in contributing?'

'Contributing what?'

'Well, your point of view.'

'My point of view on what?'

'Well anything that's relevant to the area. For example, what do you think of your local council?'

'Well, it's my view that the council are a bunch of self-serving idiots.'

'Really?'

'Really.'

'Well, unfortunately those sorts of comments are not uncommon but we can't publish them. May I come in?'

'No.'

'Right, but I do think you'll be disappointed.'

'Why should I be?'

'Well, a beautiful cottage like this deserves a special mention. We could do a write-up on it and take photographs. It would be a great treat for you and for all our readers, especially if you allowed us indoors. I myself am particularly interested in antiques and I'm sure you have plenty of those.'

Ruby hesitated. She was always vulnerable to flattering remarks about her beloved cottage but Archie had warned her about this Leggit.

'Aren't you one of the people pushing for this housing scheme on The Meadow?

The councillor feigned amnesia. 'The housing scheme on the meadow, you say? ... now let me see ... we have had so many applications lately.'

'You did say you were a councillor?' said Ruby.

'Yes, that is so.'

'Then it should come as no surprise to you to know we have an area called The Meadow. You just passed it on the way up here.'

'Of course I know it. You were referring to *that* Meadow. There are so many of them round here.'

'Yes, I mean *that* Meadow. So are you pushing for houses there?'

'I wouldn't say *pushing* no. Not exactly *pushing*. In fact, as I recall it, that scheme is in abeyance at the moment because no planning consent has been granted yet. There is a long process ahead so I wouldn't worry if I were you. Anyway, if I may get back to the purpose of my visit, are you sure you don't want to talk about your lovely cottage and its history?'

'Well, I am rather busy right now. Come back when my nephew's in and talk to him.'

'I too am rather busy. But never mind, there may be other opportunities but unfortunately too late for our first issue.'

'Very well, I'll give you two minutes,' said Ruby 'and that's all.'

Councillor Leggit gave himself a mental pat on the back. He knew that if you poured enough oil on, the wheels would begin to turn.

'Thank you, that's most helpful. Er, my researchers tell me the cottage has been in the Manning family for a long time. Is that true?'

'Yes. Fred's father and grandfather lived here.'

'And you started living here about forty odd years ago?'

'So you know already?'

'Only because I did a little research.'

'I see. Yes, I have been living here about that long.'

'And then your partner died fairly recently?'

'My *husband* died recently, yes.'

'Oh your *husband*! Forgive me, I didn't realise. I did search the archives for evidence of a marriage certificate, but I'm afraid I couldn't find one.'

'Really? Are you saying we were not married then?' There was a marked chill in Ruby's tone.

'No, no, not at all dear lady. I'm merely saying I couldn't find the evidence.'

'Really. Where did you look?'

'Well the registrar's office of course. The national archives in London. They keep records of all the marriages in this country.'

'So, therefore you think we were not married. That we lived together but were not married?'

'No, I didn't say that.'

'But that's what you meant.'

'Dear lady, please! I'm only trying to gather a few facts.'

'Right, well if you'll wait a moment, I have something to show you.'

She came back a few seconds later with her shotgun. The councillor eyed it nervously. 'Now hold on a moment,' he said. 'You just can't go around shooting people.'

'What a suggestion!' said Ruby. 'I thought you said you were interested in antiques?'

'I am.'

'Well, there you are then. I'm just showing you one of my antiques. Anyway, now you've seen it, you can go.'

'Thanks, I think I will,' said the councillor, turning away.

'Oh, and by the way, 'she said, 'Fred and I were married, but you should have done your homework properly. We were married in Scotland.'

The councillor gaped, momentarily deprived of speech.

'Well, have you nothing to say?' she said, suddenly angry as she waved the gun in the air.

He was moving at a brisk pace when the door slammed behind him.

14

'I've just been talking to Maisie Albright,' Ruby announced as she returned from a visit to the village shop.

Archie looked up from reading a copy of *The Evesbury Echo*. 'It says here that you should never talk to tall, dark strangers.'

'What?'

'I've just been reading your horoscope in *The Echo*. It contains the aforementioned advice.'

'Well, it's wrong on three counts. Maisie isn't tall or dark and she's no stranger.'

'I'll write to the editor. Can't have them printing this sort of guff. So who is this Maisie?'

'Archie!' said Ruby, beginning to unload her shopping basket. 'You know very well who she is. I introduced you to her at The Ladies Club.'

'Did you? Well, it's not surprising I can't remember. There were rather a lot of them.'

'But you must remember her. Blonde and rather pretty.'

'Oh, of course, that one! For some reason, I've been thinking of her as Marilyn. Must be mixing her up with some other blonde.'

'Anyway, the point is, I was telling her about the break-in we had and she thinks she knows who did it!'

'Does she? Well, we all know who did it don't we? At least we can guess with near certainty that it was our friend Bradley.'

'Yes, Bradley was behind it, but she means the actual burglar. The one who broke in.'

'Really? So who was it?'

'Ah, that's when she came over all mysterious. She thinks she knows who, but she'd like your opinion. She wants you to go along to The Highwayman in Evesbury tonight and all will be revealed.'

'Sounds like an offer I can't refuse. So you think I ought to go?'

'Well, of course, you should go Archibald. It's Singalong night and you should enjoy it. Mind you, watch out for Maisie. She's a nice girl but she is a bit of a flirt. I suspect she's on the lookout for a man.'

'Now you tell me.'

'Don't worry, she'll be too busy behind the bar to make a nuisance of herself.'

'Will she? Well, she'll be in the right place for male attention.'

'Yes, but her main job is at the riding school in Evesbury. She only helps out in the pub in the evenings.'

'I see. From mucking out to mucking in.'

'Something like that. Anyway, I hope she's got some good information for you.'

'Every little helps,' said Archie.

The Highwayman had already attracted a number of customers when Archie entered. Tables were filling up and several already had drinks in front of them. Some were standing in a group at one end of the bar while others sat on stools in front of it. He took a good look round and decided to join the line of lone wolves perched on stools. He found a vacant spot between a moustached military-looking type sipping what looked like a whisky and a serious-looking chap with a pint of ale. Behind the bar, Archie saw the blonde head of the girl he recognised as

Maisie. She was bending over a pint pot and pulling on the pump handle.

'Can we expect some good music tonight then?' he enquired of the military type.

'Depends on your taste. Not my sort of stuff but at least it's cheerful. Put it this way, it beats sitting in an armchair listening to my landlady going on about her rheumatics.'

'A fair point,' said Archie. 'Landladies and rheumatics seem to go together. It must be all that rising damp.'

On the other side of Archie, the mournful chap said, 'You'll enjoy it mate. It gets better as the night goes on.'

'The entertainment?'

'And the beer.'

'You'd recommend it then?'

'Yeah, it's a good pint.'

'Does it have a name?'

'Course it does. It's Sham and Aubrey's best bitter.'

'Sounds good. Same again for you?'

'Ta.'

'I'm Archie by the way.' He held out his hand.

'Les', said the other as they shook hands. 'Les Corkhill, though I'm usually known as Corky.'

'Good to meet you Corky.' Archie turned to his other companion. 'How about you, er ...'

'Mike ... Mike Chislehurst.'

'Archie Graham.' They shook hands.

'Thanks, that's very civil of you. Whisky and soda please.'

'I'm guessing you're in the army,' said Archie.

'What makes you say that?'

'Something to do with the military bearing I think.'

'Well you're half right. I was a Major but now I'm plain mister.'

'I see. Well, you still look very much the part.'

'And always will, I suppose. What about the moustache?'

'What about it?'

'Well it suited me in the military I suppose, but now I'm thinking of shaving it off.'

'Oh, any particular reason?'

'I'd like to get married. Anything to escape Mrs Gibbs.'

'Mrs Gibbs?'

'The landlady.'

'Ah, I see. And you think losing the moustache might help?'

'Well, it's not done much for me so far.'

'Good point.'

'What can I get you?' said a new voice.

Archie looked up to see Maisie standing before him with a friendly smile.

'Oh hello,' he said, returning the smile. 'A whisky and soda please, and two pints of Sham and Thingy's bitter.'

'Sham and Aubrey's.'

'That's the one. I'm told it's good.'

'Well everybody says so. It's a guest beer.'

'Yeah,' said Corky, 'One sip and you've guessed it's beer!' He let out a honking sort of laugh.

'Hilarious,' said Archie,

The captain rolled his eyes. 'He cracked that one last week and probably the week before.'

As Maisie went off, Archie said, 'Why don't you ask her about moustaches? She's bound to have an opinion.'

The Major pondered a moment. 'If you're sure she won't take offence.'

'I don't think she's the type.'

'Would you ask her for me?'

'I will if she's not too busy. She seems to be all on her own.'

'Yeah,' said Corky. 'The landlord's gone down with the flu. I did offer to 'elp for the price of a couple of pints, but she reckoned she could manage.'

'Shame,' said Archie, 'but she does seem to be coping.'

When Maisie came back with the drinks, she said, 'I've opened a tab for you Archie. Is that okay?'

'Fine. And while you're here you can settle an argument for us.'

'What's that then?'

'The question is, do ladies go for men with moustaches?'

She thought a moment. 'It's hard to say. It really depends on the man. Let's see ... George and Pierre ... oh and Steve, they all had moustaches. On the other hand, there was Will, who was smooth and, er, do you want me to include yourself in this survey?'

'No, no, that's fine,' said Archie, hurriedly. 'I think we understand. Thanks anyway.'

'Any time,' she said with a grin. 'See you later.' She went off.

At that moment there was a burst of applause. Archie looked up to see a small slim figure emerge from a door marked 'Private'. On his shoulder sat a monkey with a red fez on its head. Although the man was small, Archie could see that he had strength and grace.

'That's Gino,' said Corky. He plays the pianner and everybody sings.'

'Or tries,' said the Major, 'but he doesn't so much play the instrument as attack it.'

'It's a wonder he got past the audition.'

'Quite easily, I think. He was hired by the landlord who happens to be tone deaf.'

'Well I like 'im,' said Corky, 'and so do the other customers.'

'Well, they do say the customer is always right,' said the Major.

'Looks like the landlord was right too,' said Archie. 'The place is packed.'

As Gino bowed and sat down at the piano, the captain produced an ear plug and stuck it in his left ear. 'Just protecting the good ear,' he explained in a voice louder than usual. 'I'm deaf in the other one. That's why I got chucked out of the army.'

'Should we use sign language then?' asked Archie.

'Pardon?'

'Never mind. I think the festivities are about to begin.'

Gino had seated himself at the piano while the monkey sat on top. With a theatrical flourish, the maestro raised his hands and brought them crashing down on the keyboard. Archie had seldom heard a row like it. He turned to Corky, and raised his voice. 'Does he always play like this?' he enquired.

'Oh, yeah,' said Corky. 'Good innit?'

Archie turned to the Major. Pointing at his ear, he mouthed, 'Has it done the trick?'

The captain removed the plug. 'Pardon?'

'The plug. Does it stop the noise?'

'Yes it does, but only when it's in the ear.'

'Ah, yes. Good point. Anyway, now that you can hear me, what's your opinion of the music? I'm told it's quite difficult to play the piano badly. You have to be able to play a piece properly before deliberately messing it up.'

'He's not deliberately messing it up. He always plays like that.' With that he stuck the plug back in his ear.

'What's he supposed to be playing?' Archie said to Corky.

'A bit of classical. He always starts with a bit of classical.'

'Which bit of classical is it?'

'Dunno. Probably 'andle or summat.'

At that moment the overture came to an end and the maestro produced a piece of cardboard with the word REQWESTS written on it. A cheer went up as it was held up and voices began to shout out various song titles. After a moment, Gino put his hand up for silence and turned back to the piano. Soon, songs were being belted out by the massed choirs of the lounge and public bar who seemed to know what he was playing. Old favourites such as 'Roll Out The Barrel' and 'She'll Be Comin' Round The Mountain' were shaking the foundations and there was general mayhem when 'Under The Spreading Chestnut Tree' was accompanied by the actions. Arms flailed about and a lot of beer was spilt.

'Everybody seems to be having fun,' said Archie to his mournful neighbour.

'Told yer,' said Corky, swaying to the music and slopping his beer around while they watched the monkey. It was darting through the crowd collecting money in the fez.

So the evening went on and it came as something of a shock when the bell was rung for last orders. There was a concerted rush to the bar and Maisie was soon working feverishly to cope. Shortly after there was a maudlin rendition of 'Show Me The Way To Go Home' before Gino stood up to take a final bow. He then collected the monkey, waved and made his way out through the door marked 'Private,' followed by loud cheers.

After a few more minutes of drinking-up time, final farewells were being said and there was a gradual drift towards the door. Archie and his two companions stood up, ready to move off.

Archie held out a hand to the Major. 'G'night Major.' he said. 'Keep lookin' for the right girl, but take my advice. Avoid the ones with moustaches.'

'Good advice,' said the Major, seemingly unaffected by the

amount of whisky he'd consumed. He saluted, set his face to-wards the door and marched steadily across the room as if to the sound of a military band.

Archie turned to his other companion. 'Okay, Corky?' he en-quired.

'Yup,' said Corky.

As they started off, they soon found it necessary to hold on to each other, owing to the fact that the floor seemed to be on the move.

'Are we at sea?' asked Archie.

'Seems like it, and in a storm an' all.'

'Archie!' It was Maisie ... 'Don't go yet. We need to talk.'

'Okay, go ahead.'

'In private, if you don't mind.'

'I don't mind,' said Archie. 'Do you mind?' he said to Corky.

'Not at all, mate. 'Tell you what, 'ave you 'eard the one about ...'

'Could you leave it till next time, Corky?' said Maisie. 'This is important.'

'But this won't take long. There was this fella ... oh all right,' said Corky catching sight of Maisie's eye. 'See yer later then.' With that he made a sudden lurch to the door, managed to open it and fell through into the night.

'Let me help you to sit down,' said Maisie, putting an arm round Archie and guiding him to the nearest chair. She sat beside him. 'Isn't this cosy?' she giggled.

Archie searched his memory for a reason for all this. 'I know,' he said suddenly. 'You know this burglar.'

'I don't actually know who it is, but I do have a strong suspi-cion. That's why I'd like your opinion.'

'Archie?'

But Archie was fast asleep.

Opening one eye, Archie looked carefully round him. He raised his head and immediately let it fall again as he felt someone attack his skull with a chipping hammer. At the same time he became aware of a figure standing over him.

'Awake at last?' said a familiar voice.

'Maisie?' he managed to mumble.

'Time for you to take a drink.'

'Eh? Donthinso.'

'What was that?'

He made an effort to untangle his vocal chords. 'Not now.'

'This isn't optional Archie. It'll help your hangover.'

'It doesn't need any help.'

'You'll have to sit up.'

'Eh?'

'Try to sit up.' He felt a hand tugging at his arm. He pushed with his feet and started moving very slowly upwards while the hammer wielders resumed their attack with renewed vigour. He felt a cup touching his lips and the next moment he was gulping down some foul tasting stuff that made him heave.

'Well done,' said Maisie. 'Look Archie, I have to get to the riding stable now. I'm late already but you should be okay. Help yourself to whatever you want for breakfast, close the door after you when you leave and I'll speak to you later.'

'Where am I?'

'In my flat. You slept on the settee.'

'Why?'

'Because you overdid things a bit last night. It's lucky I don't live far from the pub and you came round long enough to stagger here. You kept saying you wanted to get back to the cottage but I thought it best if you slept it off here first.'

'Brains as well as beauty.'

She giggled. 'You say all the right things. Well, I must be going.' She bent and gave him a kiss on the cheek before disappearing towards the stairs.

Archie flopped back on to the settee and closed his eyes. The thought of getting up held no attractions and he daren't even contemplate breakfast as suggested by Maisie. For the time being, keeping still seemed to be the best way to abate the banging in his head.

He wasn't quite sure how much time had passed when he suddenly found himself wondering why he was lounging about at this late hour.

He felt grubby and ravenous at the same time. He found her tiny bathroom and washed as best he could before clattering round the kitchen, regretting his inability to make anything more adventurous than tea, toast and jam. It was when he was on his fourth round of toast that he spotted the folded notepaper. It was stuck under a small plate on the worktop with his name printed on the outside. Opening it, he read:

Archie,

We didn't get a chance to talk last night but I was rather busy! Could you give me a call ASAP (Ruby has my number).

Love. Maisie X

She'd signed off as though they'd been friends for years, he thought. But that was Maisie. He decided he'd do as she asked and get in touch later. Meanwhile, it was time to get back to the cottage and sort himself out.

15

Ruby eyed him with some amusement. 'You look a bit rumpled,' she observed.

'Yes, I need a shave and a change of clothes.'

'I'll heat some water. So have you solved the mystery then?'

'No, I'm afraid not. Maisie was too busy to talk last night but she wants to see me again.'

'I'm not surprised. I think she has her eye on you.'

'Well, she hadn't time to say much last night because the landlord was down with the flu and there was quite a crowd, all shouting for attention.'

'Couldn't you have talked after closing?'

'Not really. I was er, rather tired by then so I stayed over.'

'I won't ask for details. I'm just glad you didn't try driving home while you were under the influence.'

'Who said I was under the influence?'

'I did, but say no more. You're not a teenager now.'

'I hope you weren't worried.'

'I always worry, Archibald. It was the same when Fred was a bit late getting home. But I always knew he would turn up eventually and I felt the same about you last night.'

'Well that's nice to know. Anyway, what are we doing today?'

'There's not much we can do. Perhaps we could have a look in Fred's old shed in case it needs sorting out. Up to now, I haven't had the heart to go near it.'

'Don't you keep the garden tools in there?'

'We were both keen gardeners, Archibald, so we had our own

tools. I always keep mine in the outhouse.'

'Yes,' muttered Archie, fingering his forehead, 'nearly always anyway.'

'What was that?'

'Nothing, Aunt. Er, I need to nip to the phone box at some point to give Maisie a call. Other than that, I'm at your disposal.'

'Would you like anything to eat first?'

'Later, if that's okay. I'll just go and get cleaned up.'

'Right. Oh, before you go, you remember the meeting we had at The Ladies Club?'

'Will I ever forget it?'

'I've had a massage from Mildred Crouch. It seems that our MP, George Winder, has had a word with the Housing Minister at Westminster. His advice was to ask the local council to test opinion among the locals in a public meeting. George is writing to the council to that effect.'

'Really? Wonders will never cease.'

The shed was quite a big affair and Archie remembered it as being something of a refuge for his uncle. It was the ideal spot to unwind after a day of dealing with the unruly elements that seemed to infest even a quiet part of the country like this. This need for solitude wasn't always because of his job. Sometimes when he'd incurred Ruby's wrath, Fred would seek sanctuary here until the storm had passed.

Ruby led the way to the shed as far as the door. 'This is the first time I've been here since he went,' she said sadly, 'and I don't think I can face it. You'll have to do it on your own if you don't mind.' With that, she suddenly turned and fled back to the house. Archie stayed silent as she disappeared inside, feeling that there was nothing to be said. After a moment, he opened the shed door and went in.

He'd been there once before to collect Fred's fishing gear but he hadn't taken much notice. Now he had a good look round. The air smelled strongly of fertiliser mingled with the faint scent of pipe tobacco. In one wall there was a window looking out onto the nearby Meadow with trees and the river beyond. Under the window was a bench with various bits and pieces associated with potting up and there was an old primus stove with a couple of murky-looking mugs alongside. Tools hung from brackets on all sides. Bags of compost and fertiliser were stacked around together with all the usual paraphernalia of a garden shed. In front of the bench was a swivel chair of the kind usually occupied by the executives of large companies. Archie remembered it being bought by Fred in a local fire sale. All in all, it seemed like a very comfortable retreat.

Under the bench, there were built-in cupboards on either side. In one, there were shelves of woodworking tools of various kinds. In the other, he saw a couple of unopened bottles of pale ale and a small collection of books. It looked as if Fred took his leisure time seriously. Archie took out the bottles and put them on one side with the thought that, with his aunt's approval, they might drink to Fred's memory one evening. He looked with interest at the books.

There was a small collection of crime stories, a copy of Roget's Thesaurus and a tattered copy of Treasures of English Verse. It was, Archie realised, an insight into his uncle's tastes that he had never suspected before. Fred was apparently keen to improve his knowledge of words, read poetry and lose himself in the fictional world where crimes, unlike the ones he dealt with, were all happily solved.

In addition, there was a black notebook. Inside there were various jottings in Fred's rather crabbed handwriting. Archie started to read, feeling a bit guilty as if he was intruding on his uncle's privacy. He soon realised that what he was looking at was not an official notebook, but a list of Fred's private thoughts and opinions on the people he had to deal with as a policeman.

There were no names, only initials. Alongside each set of initials were some brief notes about each individual. So EP for instance, was caught shoplifting. 'Not a habitual criminal,' according to Fred. On the other hand, there was DD who was down as 'a local villain.' He'd been arrested for housebreaking and was 'as nasty as they come.' Then there was RK, who'd been cautioned for disturbing the peace. 'One to watch,' was Fred's cryptic note. Archie reflected that it was this meticulous approach that had made Fred such a successful bobby.

He was about to close the book when some other initials caught his eye. He read the entry with interest. 'JB (builder) – Garage – SP? Cora?'

'JB' must be Joe Bradley, mused Archie, and it was clear that Fred suspected him of some wrongdoing, but what? What did 'SP' and Cora mean? And what did they have to do with his garage? Archie decided that this merited further investigation. That decided, he closed the book, put it back where he found it and headed off to the cottage.

Ruby, it turned out, was able to put names to most of the initials. She thought DD stood for Danny Dooley, arrested by Fred in the past and now working for Bradley. 'I'm sure it was Dooley outside the cottage trying to scare me,' she said. 'The only one I can't work out is SP. I don't know anyone with those initials, unless you include Samuel Pepys.'

'Probably not,' said Archie. 'Too busy writing his diaries.'

They sat in silence for a moment.

'Okay,' Archie said, eventually. 'What about this Cora? Can

you throw any light on that?'

'Ah, yes!' said Ruby. 'That probably refers to the so-called Cora necklace.'

Archie raised an eyebrow. 'Cora necklace? I'm still none the wiser.'

'Of course, you're not. It's almost a year ago now and you weren't here.' She paused, frowning.

'Go on,' said Archie encouragingly. 'Tell me about Cora. Who is she and what happened to her necklace?'

Ruby nodded. 'I remember Fred's interest in it. It was a burglary on his patch and he had a strong suspicion that Joe Bradley was behind it. He would have liked to pursue the case but, not surprisingly, it was handed over to the local CID. Not that they managed to solve it,' she added tartly.

'So, this Cora, whoever she is, had her necklace pinched?'

'That's right. She's married to a wealthy businessman, called Charlie Fryer and they live in a big house called "The Mount" about half a mile from here. Anyway, Cora was a bit careless with her jewellery. Instead of locking it away when not in use, she'd sling it in a drawer in her bedroom.'

'And somebody broke in and pinched it?'

'How do you know?'

'Just a wild guess.'

'Anyway, there was a big hoo-ha about it when the insurance company refused to pay up because the jewellery wasn't kept in a safe place. It was even reported in the national newspapers.'

'I see,' said Archie. 'So Fred's notes could refer to his suspicions about Bradley being behind the burglary?'

'Yes. You see Bradley and his gang had been working on the house for some weeks beforehand, doing repairs and painting and decorating and so on. Then they left and the burglary happened a couple of weeks later. Naturally, they were questioned but nothing came of it and Bradley himself had a cast-iron alibi for the night the deed was done.'

'Trust him. That in itself is suspicious. He'd made sure he could not be implicated.'

'Fred said exactly the same thing. Anyway, enough of that for now. How about a cup of tea and a slice of homemade cake?'

16

As he entered The Highwayman Archie cast a wary glance at the floor. At least it seemed to have stopped moving since he was last here. It was lunchtime and there was a scattering of customers seated around the room. He spotted Maisie fulfilling her role behind the bar and she treated him to her usual warm smile. 'Be with you in a minute,' she said, as she completed an order for a red-faced chap in tweeds. Archie seated himself at the bar and wondered if Corky would put in an appearance after the previous night's indulgences. 'If he feels the same as I felt,' he thought, 'probably not.'

Maisie finished with the red-faced chap and came down the bar. 'Archie!' she said. 'Feeling better?'

'Much better thanks. That mixture of yours was nothing short of miraculous. You should patent it. Still on your own I see.'

'Yeah. I think it'll be a few more days before Bert recovers.'

'You've finished your morning stint at the stables then?'

'They let me go early, knowing the situation here. You wouldn't like to help out would you?'

'What, behind the bar?'

'No, at the stables.'

'Not me. I don't know one end of a horse from the other.'

'Pity. I think you'd look good in riding gear.'

'If you don't mind, I think I'll stick to the car. It's easier to steer.'

She giggled. 'Would you like a drink?'

'Nothing alcoholic,' he assured her. 'It does terrible things to you.'

'What'll it be then?'

'I'll have a glass of your finest tap water, if that's okay.'

'We're not going to get fat on your profits,' she said as she filled a glass.

'I boosted the profits last night though. And by the way, I owe you one for putting up with me.'

'It was my pleasure,' she said, looking slightly pink around the cheeks. She suddenly noticed the red-faced chap leaning towards them with his ears flapping. 'Anyway,' she said, lowering her voice to a whisper, 'I wanted to talk to you about these burglaries. I have a suspicion about who might be involved.'

'Okay. So who is the guilty party?'

'You saw him last night. Gino, the pianist.' She said this in a whisper.

Archie looked astonished. 'Really?'

'I think so. 'And keep your voice down,' she said with a sideways glance.

'Gotcha.'

'Gino works for Joe Bradley and I'm sure there's something going on there. It's not just Ruby's cottage. There've been a few break-ins in town just lately and it looks as if it's the same person. Whoever it is can get in through the smallest of openings and that's where I think Gino and his monkey come in. They used to work in a circus together and that monkey is well trained.'

'I see. And do you think Gino is doing it for Bradley's benefit?'

'I think so. He hasn't said so in so many words but I can read between the lines. Gino is a bag of nerves when it comes to Bradley and I'm sure Bradley has some sort of hold over him.'

'So you think Gino is being forced into this?'

'I think so. In fact I'm almost sure so.'

'So you'd like me to have a word with him?'

'Yes please. He's in the back.'

'Does he know I'm coming to talk to him?'

'Of course not, he'd probably run a mile. He thinks he's here just to collect his share of the profits from last night. I left him sitting in the back with a sandwich and a drink.'

'Okay,' said Archie, raising his voice slightly, 'let's talk privately before the chap at the end of the bar falls off his stool.'

'Follow me,' said Maisie, as the red-faced chap shot upright, harrumphed and pretended to study the artwork on a beer mat.

In the back room, Gino was sitting nervously on the edge of a chair. He eyed Archie suspiciously.

'Gino,' said Maisie, 'had enough to eat?'

'T'ank you Maisie, yourra very kind.'

'Not at all. I'd like you to meet a friend of mine. Archie meet Gino.'

Archie held out a hand. Gino looked at it as if it was an unexploded grenade before giving it a limp handshake.

'So where's the monkey today, Gino?' Archie asked chattily.

'Peppi is wit' Mrs O'Hara.'

'Mrs O'Hara is Gino's landlady,' explained Maisie helpfully.

'Landlady eh? She doesn't happen to suffer from rheumatics does she?'

'Eh?'

'Never mind. It's okay Gino,' said Archie, seating himself in a nearby chair. 'I just wanted to meet you. I was here last night when you, er, played the piano.'

Gino relaxed slightly, looking pleased. 'It good huh?'

'I can honestly say I've never heard anything like it.'

'Heh! Everybody happy huh?'

'I don't know how you do it.'

'He's used to entertaining people. Been in show business for years,' said Maisie. 'In Italy. Look, can I leave you two together? I have to get back to the bar.'

'Of course,' said Archie, 'but before you go, do either of you know anyone with the initials SP?'

Their blank faces told Archie all he wanted to know. 'Okay,' he said finally, 'just keep thinking about it and let me know if you come up with anything.'

When Maisie had gone, Archie turned to Gino. 'Sounds like you've had an interesting career, Gino. What sort of show business were you in then?'

'I was in de circus,' Gino said proudly. 'Trapeze, high wire, any'ting like dat.'

'Wow! Just in Italy?'

'Sure. But we go plenty other places also.'

'So you went touring. Did you tour this country?'

'Sure. It how I come here. But den de circus ... it how you say? ... go bang.'

'Bang? You mean it went bust? So you all got laid off?'

'Eh?'

'You got the sack ... the bum's rush?'

'*Si*. We all get sack so I take Peppi and look for job.'

'Is that when you started working for Bradley?'

Gino's face fell and his sunny mood suddenly evaporated. 'Si,

I work for Bradley.'

'Cheer up,' said Archie. 'Worse things happen at sea.'

'Eh?'

'At least you've got a job.'

'Oh sure, but it don't do me no good. He not a good man.'

'Yes, I think we all know that. So, is he making you do something you don't like?'

Gino looked even sadder. 'He on to me all de time.'

'You could leave. Get another job.'

'Yeah?' He heaved a sigh. 'I don't have no choice.'

'There's always a choice.'

'Not for me.'

'Why not? Has he got some sort of hold over you?'

'Say!' said Gino, suddenly suspicious, 'you're notta de police are you?'

'No I'm notta, er not. So what's made you afraid of Bradley?'

Gino tried to look outraged but didn't quite succeed. 'What makes you t'ink I afraid, huh?' He suddenly got to his feet. 'Anyway, I gotta go.' He took a step towards the door.

Archie regarded him with something near to despair. For someone with nerves of steel at thirty feet, Gino was nothing but a jelly at ground level. The nice guy approach didn't seem to be working with him, so perhaps it was time to take a tougher line. He took a couple of quick steps to stand in front of the door, cutting off the little man's escape route.

'Isn't it about time you pulled yourself together?' he asked in a sterner tone.

'Eh?'

'You seem to be in mortal fear of Bradley, so why don't you get it off your chest and tell somebody what's going on?'

'Who I tell?'

'Me and right now!'

Gino hesitated, looking as if he'd been slapped in the face with a something off the fish counter. His mouth opened and closed a few times before he slumped back in his seat. He put his head in his hands. 'It true,' he moaned. 'It's a mess and I ain't got a clue what to do.'

'Okay,' said Archie, keeping up his hectoring tone. 'Just tell me.'

'You sure you notta the police?'

'I've already told you, I'm just a friend of Maisie's.'

'Okay, okay.' Gino's defences seemed suddenly to collapse and the story came pouring out. His job with Bradley had been fine for a while. Poorly paid but better than nothing, he said. He was popular with the men because of the speedy way he fetched and carried stuff for them, moving up and down scaffolding with the agility of a chimpanzee. Sometimes he would entertain them during a break with a demonstration of his circus skills. He could throw himself around juggling a variety of small objects at the same time. And, if he knew Bradley was going to be away, he would sometimes introduce Peppi as part of the act.

Things started to go wrong when he was called into the office one day and grilled about his status. Bradley accused him of being an illegal immigrant while Gino protested he had a visa. But, as they both knew, the visa had passed its expiry date. At this point, Bradley became sympathetic and told him not to worry. So long as he followed orders, said the builder, he'd be okay.

Gino's relief at this turned out to be short-lived when he next learned what his orders were to be.

'He wanted you to burgle houses?'

'Si ... Hey, how you know this?'

'Just a guess. There's been a few burglaries round here recently and no one's been caught. So what did you say?'

'I tell him I can't do it. It not honest.'

'And what did he say to that?'

'He ask me did I think staying in a country illegally was honest. I don't have no answer to dat.'

'And he threatened to report you if you didn't do what he wanted?'

'Yeah, you got it.'

'Okay Gino, tell me more.'

'Bradley's workers know what he is like. They know he's a crook.' 'He took on a lad called Gary who'd been done for shoplifting. The next thing Gary was shoplifting again on Bradley's behalf. In the end Gary got on his bike and disappeared to some other part of the country.'

This made Archie think. His uncle Fred had made reference to a Gary in his little book of suspects. It confirmed that Fred was keeping a close eye on what Bradley and his lot were doing. 'Interesting,' he muttered to himself. Out loud, he said, 'Thanks Gino. So it must have been you who broke into my aunt's cottage and took some papers?'

Gino looked shamefaced. 'Hey, I very sorry bout dat. He make me do it.'

'I guessed that,' said Archie, 'you didn't pinch anything valuable, and we think we know what he was looking for. He didn't find it, but that's another story.'

'Hey, I just do what he tell me. To look in dat chest and take what's inside. I don know how he knew there was papers in der.'

'It's okay. I think I know the answer to that one too.'

Archie stepped out of the way of the door. 'Okay, cheer up Gino, you've done the right thing,' he said. 'We'll keep in touch.'

He held out his hand. The little man gave Archie one of his trademark wet lettuce handshakes. 'I 'ope so,' he said as made a mournful exit.

17

'The plot thickens,' said Archie, as he sipped his tea. 'Maisie introduced me to the man who burgled this place.'

'What!' said Ruby, stopping in the middle of arranging flowers, 'are you serious?'

'Perfectly. Mind you, it was only my suspicion to start with, but he eventually admitted it.'

'Well, go on then. Tell me about it.'

'I don't think the name will mean anything to you. He's called Gino and he works for Bradley.'

'I might have known he was behind it.'

'According to Gino, Bradley not only masterminded this one, but other local burglaries as well.'

Ruby gave a little jig. 'Archibald! You're a genius!' She came over and kissed his cheek. 'This means we can get Bradley arrested, and that'll put an end to all this housing nonsense.'

'I'd like to do what you suggest but it's not as simple as that. Gino would only talk when he was sure we wouldn't involve the police. That would get him arrested too.'

Ruby looked disappointed. 'You gave him your word?'

'I'm afraid so.'

She sighed. 'Ah well! We'll just have to find another way. Why does he want places burgled anyway?'

'Just straightforward greed for more money, I suppose. Anyway, I'm going out shortly to meet Al Richards. He's told Bradley that he's got a potential buyer for some of his houses on this Meadow development. Bradley's apparently eager, so he'll be at Al's pub this afternoon. We're ready to put on a bit of a performance for him. I'll be posing as a *Monsieur* Pierre Tatti, a wealthy French investor, interested in buying several properties.'

'You're posing as a Frenchman?'

'Well mainly an investor, but by posing as a foreigner too, I can always pretend not to understand something. Do I look like a Frenchman, by the way?'

'I don't know, I haven't met any.'

'Well, broadly they look the same as us but perhaps with a tendency to moustaches and hats.'

'You can borrow Fred's best trilby. Anyway, what are you hoping to get out of it?'

'Oh, just to learn a bit more about this Bradley. I like to know who I'm dealing with ... or should that be, with whom I am dealing?'

Ruby sniffed. 'It all sounds risky to me, Archibald.'

'I don't think so. Even if he rumbles me, what's he going to do about it? He's not the sort to go running to the police is he? Not when he's got so much to hide himself.'

'But what about Al?'

'Well, Al's prepared for anything. He'll claim that he was as much fooled by me as Bradley was. He knows he's risking the sack, but he's ready to take retirement anyway, so he's not bothered. He just loves the idea of getting one over on Bradley.'

'I see. Just be careful then.'

'Scout's honour.'

'And I didn't know you spoke French.'

'I don't. Not unless you count the schoolboy variety. But I do a very good Gallic shrug.'

Archie stood in the doorway of the Blue Barrel and looked round. He saw Al Richards was seated at the table in his usual corner and with him was a beanpole figure looking distinctly uncomfortable in a blue suit. He was periodically running his finger round his collar to ease the unfamiliar constriction of a collar and tie. So Bradley had dressed up for the occasion. Good! thought Archie, he wants to make an impression. As he crossed over to the couple, Al spotted him and stood up. Archie held out his arms.

'Ah! *Monsieur* Al,' he cried, embracing him and air-kissing him on both cheeks. 'So, 'ow are you, *mon ami*?'

'Very well, Pierre. Er, may I introduce Mister Joseph Bradley, the builder.' Bradley had been watching the scene warily. He shook Archie's outstretched hand, making sure he was out of hugging range.

'Can I get you a drink, Pierre?' Asked Al.

'*Merci*, but I 'ave not much time, you know?' said Archie, sounding like a bad actor in a B movie. 'I 'ave a very busy day ahead.'

'Well sit down anyway and take the weight off your feet.'

Archie removed his hat, which had been resting on his ears, and sat.

'Joe, *Monsieur* Tatti would like a bit of information about your scheme so he can decide if it's a worthwhile investment,' said Al.

Bradley summoned up an ingratiating grin. 'Of course, it's a great investment opportunity. *Avez vous une bonne idée de quel type d'endroit vous cherchez*?' he asked.

Archie gaped.

'*Y a-t-il un problèm monsieur*?' the builder enquired.

Archie recovered sufficiently to give a Gallic shrug. 'Er, Joe,' said Al hastily. 'I asked *Monsieur* Tatti if he'd mind if we only spoke English in our conversation so I could follow it. He told me that was fine by him as he wants to practise his English anyway.'

Bradley looked disappointed. 'Oh, right,' was all he said.

'Any questions?' said Al.

'Yes,' said Archie, managing to gather his scattered wits. 'What about the permission? You 'ave this?'

'He means planning permission,' said Al helpfully.

'It's on the way,' said Bradley. 'Just a formality,' he added.

Archie frowned at the builder. 'You 'ave no permission yet? So what does this mean?'

'Nothing to worry about,' Bradley assured him. 'It'll come through any day now.'

'You're sure of zis?'

'Sure I'm sure.'

'Joe has connections,' said Al.

'Do you mind letting me handle this?' said Bradley, directing a glare at him. 'Yes, as a matter of fact I happen to know that the planning committee, who control these matters, are in favour of the scheme.'

'Joe is a good friend of the chairman,' said Al.

Bradley pulled at his collar again. 'Shouldn't you be back on the job?' he snarled. That house in Batty Street should have been finished by now.'

'You're the boss,' said Al, getting to his feet. 'Looks as if I'll have to say goodbye to you, Pierre,' he said as they shook hands. 'Be seeing you.'

'Soon, I 'ope,' said Archie, as Al disappeared though the door. '*Au Revoir mon ami!*'

'A verra nice man, *n'est pas*?'

'He has his uses,' said Bradley. 'Now, perhaps we can get down to business.'

'Only if I can be sure eet is good business.'

'Oh, no question about it ... quality housing, riverside location. You can't go wrong! So how many were you considering buying?'

'I cannot say at this stage, *monsieur*. First I must be sure you 'ave the necessary permission and then I must check the quality of your 'ouses.'

Bradley stared. 'Check them? They're not built yet.'

'Of course, but you 'ave built 'ouses before?'

'Of course. That's what I do.'

'Quite so, *monsieur*. So I will look at one or two of those.'

Bradley fingered his collar. 'I'm afraid that won't be possible. They are all occupied and I don't think the owners would like a stranger wandering about the place.'

'Quite so, but inspection will not be necessary. A chat with ze owners will suffice. If you will give me some addresses, I will call on them and if zey are pleased with your work zen I will be 'appy.'

The builder did not reply immediately. He'd been trying to assert himself in this conversation but it was proving difficult. The idea of someone asking one of his old clients for comments on a home he'd built was unsettling. He was no stranger to the dozens of petty complaints people made about shoddy and poor quality work. 'Okay, I'll try and arrange something,' he said, his mind already working on how he could get round this one.

'*Bon*,' said Archie, 'so that just leaves ze question of planning. I believe there 'ave been objections in ze pepper.'

'The pepper? Oh you mean *The Echo*. I wouldn't take any notice of that if I were you. It publishes all sorts of rubbish in an effort to sell more copies.'

'But I hear the old lady in ze cottage nearby is objecting very strongly.'

Bradley could not resist a sneer. 'She's just a batty old woman who doesn't like change. She won't be a problem.'

'Really?' said Archie. 'So what do you intend to do about 'er?'

'I'll do whatever it takes. Like I say, there's no need to worry. Now, can we get back to the investment? Are you ready to secure some property now?'

'Not yet, monsieur. I am a businessman and zer are too many, as you say, loose ends. And now, I too must go. I 'ave already stayed too long.' With that, Archie stood up, bowed and gathered up his hat before making his way rapidly through the bar and out of the door.

Bradley watched him go with a scowl and a few basic words in both French and English.

18

Councillor Leggit had decided to take the bull by the horns and try to resolve the dispute with the owner of Oak Tree Cottage. On his last visit, he had the uncomfortable experience of being hurried off the premises at the wrong end of a shotgun. This time he had two reasons for feeling more confident. First, he had an offer to make which he thought would appeal to gun-toting Ruby, and secondly he was wearing a bullet proof vest.

The councillor had an office in the headquarters building known as Pilbeam House. The Victorian house, standing in extensive grounds, had been built by a wealthy coal merchant named Silas Pilbeam. He was the last of a long line of Pilbeams and after him, the hall passed through a number of hands before being taken over by the council.

On a recent weekend, the house had been loaned to the army and local constabulary to rehearse certain secret manoeuvres organised by the Home Office. What these were all about was unclear, but when staff returned to the offices on the Monday morning, an abandoned bullet proof vest was found. Charlie Leggit immediately purloined it on the grounds that it would make further visits to Oak Tree Cottage that much safer. He now approached the cottage with the vest under his overcoat and the confidence of a man who was now bullet proof.

'Good morning, sir,' he said, when Archie answered the door. 'I'm Councillor Charles Leggit and I'm just calling to let Mrs Manning know that I have some good news for her. May I come in?'

'Leggit eh? I remember my aunt mentioned your name only the other day and she didn't sound too pleased.'

'Er, yes, I did call but I'm afraid there was a slight misunderstanding.'

'What, she misunderstood you or you misunderstood her?'

'I think we misunderstood each other.'

'Oh, I see. So there was a misunderstanding on both sides?'

'Exactly. I could clear it up if I had a word with her.'

'Is that wise? She was deeply upset by some of the things you said.'

'That's why I'd like a word with her. To clear up any ...'

'Misunderstanding ... yes, I think I've got that. Well, if you'll just wait there a moment, I'll see if she's ready to talk to you.'

'Thank you very much Mr er ...'

'Graham. I'm her nephew. Are you insured for personal injury by the way?'

'Oh, I don't think there's any need for anything of that nature. Especially when she hears what I have to say.'

'I think it'll be more a case of *you* hearing what *she* has to say. Anyway, hang on while I pop in and see her. She's in the kitchen, clearing up after baking. The rolling pin is already back in the drawer, you'll be glad to hear.' He disappeared inside.

The councillor stood at the door, feeling rather less comfortable than he had been. The weight of the vest was beginning to make his shoulders ache and sweat was breaking out in various unexpected places.

Archie returned to the fray. 'She says you can come in providing you wipe your feet and say what you have to say inside two minutes,' he said.

The councillor did as directed, anxious to take the weight off his feet. He was escorted to the kitchen where Ruby was wiping down the big wooden table. She eyed him with disfavour. 'What do you want?' she said.

'Good afternoon *Mrs* Manning,' he said, putting special emphasis on the 'Mrs.' 'I trust you are well?'

'Spare me the niceties,' said Ruby. 'What do you want?'

'Well, if I could just sit down for a moment, I'll be glad to explain.'

'You can explain just as well standing up.'

'Oh, very good. Well, as I was saying to Graham here, I've come to apologise and to make you an offer. A very generous offer, I might add.'

'Is that so?' said Ruby, 'Well, before you say any more, I'll thank you to have a bit more respect and address my nephew as *Mister* Graham.'

'Oh, I do apologise. I thought that was his first ...'

'Not to worry,' said Archie. 'Just another misunderstanding.'

'Well, get on with it,' said Ruby. 'Say what you have to say and then clear off.'

'Oh, yes quite.' In the warm kitchen, the sweat was beginning to pour off him. 'Well, as you already know ...'

'Never mind telling me what I already know,' said Ruby, 'just get to the point.'

'Er, yes of course. Well, I have some splendid news for you. I've found a buyer for your cottage.'

'Have you?' said Ruby. 'I don't remember asking you to find me one.'

'Well no, but you've obviously been distressed by the proposal to build houses nearby. So much so, that it seems likely you would want to move away. However, what I have found is that you can still live here without any cost to yourself.'

'Really? Well first, I've no intention of moving away and second I already live here without any cost to myself. The house is bought and paid for.'

'No, no, that's not what I mean ...'

'Then hurry up and enlighten me, I haven't got all day.' Ruby was showing signs of impatience.

'Yes, well it must be difficult living here,' said the councillor, gazing round the kitchen.

'What do you mean, difficult?'

'Well, no running water, no electricity, no main drainage and a big garden to maintain. It can't be easy for an ol ... a lady living on her own. There must be days when you wish you had something easier to look after.'

'If I were you,' said Archie, 'I'd cut out the waffle and get to the point before the rolling pin reappears.'

'Absolutely, of course Graha ... er, Mr Graham,' said the councillor. The ache in his shoulders was now much worse, he was wet with sweat and frustrated at not being allowed to approach the matter in his usual wheedling manner.

'Well, I've been talking to the builder about the proposed new housing development and he is willing to offer you one of his brand new properties in exchange for Oak Tree Cottage. What's more, he'll even pay all the legal costs. How about that?'

In the silence that ensued, the ticking of the grandfather clock in the next room sounded quite loud. It was Ruby who broke the silence.

'You hear that?' she said. 'My husband heard that tick all his life and I've listened to it for the last forty-two years. I love that sound so can you tell me what would happen to it if I moved as you suggest?'

'Er, well ...'

'I'll tell you what would happen,' she said. 'I'd have to get rid of the clock. Can you imagine how ridiculous it would look in one of those poky little rooms they have in houses nowadays? And can you imagine how my dining table would look? It probably wouldn't go through the door but even if it did, you'd have to climb over it to get to the kitchen.'

'Well ...'

'And what about the garden? This cottage stands in almost an acre of land. Do you imagine I could grow all the things I grow now, on one of those pathetic little patches?'

'Well ...'

'No, neither do I,' said Ruby. 'I've no doubt the builder would love to get his hands on this cottage so he could fit in a few more grotty little houses on my land.'

'Well ...'

'So let me make it plain to you,' said Ruby. 'I will not be moving out now or any time soon and not in fact until I'm carried out in a box fitted with polished brass handles. No, no, no. Not now, not tomorrow, not ever.'

'I don't think she's keen,' said Archie.

The councillor decided he'd had enough of this. He was now wet-through and the ache was becoming intolerable. 'Very good,' he said, 'I have other important matters to attend to so I'll be on my way.'

'Allow me to show you out,' said Archie. 'And by the way, our local MP will be asking the council to test local opinion on this housing development. He suggests a public meeting.'

The councillor looked a bit shocked by this. He paused by the door. 'I'm sure public opinion supports the provision of additional housing in this area,' he said. 'Do you not think so. Mr ... er.'

'Graham,' said Archie, 'the surname is Graham. Anyway, it's Bye for now Councillor er ... Thingy.'

'Leggit.'

'I would if I were you,' said Archie, 'before she gets the gun out again.'

19

'Are you serious?' Joe Bradley glared at the councillor.

'Of course I'm serious Joe. We have to take notice of what central government say. A lot of our funding comes from them.'

'So some pen pusher in Whitehall says "jump," and all you lot on the council can say is, "how high?"'

The pair were facing each other in Bradley's office. Councillor Leggit always felt slightly nervous in these surroundings.

'I know,' he said. 'I don't like it any more than you do, but that's the situation. George Winder, the local MP, has spoken to the Government's housing minister who advised him to test local opinion, "in the best interests of democracy," as he put it. He's written to the Mayor, asking for action along those lines. We all know the Mayor is a pretty useless sort of article of course, but he can be stubborn and he's scared of upsetting the MP, not to mention a government minister. So he's asked me, as chairman of the planning committee, to organise a consultation with local people to see if they are in favour of houses being built on The Meadow.'

'And what form is this consultation going to take?'

'Well, that's been left entirely up to me.'

'Has it? So what are you proposing to do?'

'That's what I came here to talk about. We have to find some way of organising this, not only to give us the result we want but also by way of a process that looks legitimate.'

'Why is it?' said Bradley with a malevolent look, 'why is it you seem to bring me nothing but problems? You're the one who's supposed to be in charge of all this planning business but you keep coming up with obstacles. If I hadn't already bought that field, I'd pull out of the whole thing. As it is, I'm stuck with it. And now, the one thing you can be sure of is if this thing does go ahead, you won't be getting much out of it.'

'Oh, don't be like that, Joe. It's not my fault if George Winder decided to stick his nose in. I wouldn't be surprised to find he was got at by the locals when he was in the constituency the other day. Anyway, I'm sure we'll find a way round this. We just have to be patient.'

'Patient? Try telling my bank manager that. And don't look to me to sort it out. You're the one who's supposed to be clever at solving problems, so whatever scheme you've got in mind, you need to get on with it, pronto.'

'All right Joe, I get the message. I'll come up with something, don't you worry.' He rose. 'I'll let you know as soon as I've worked it out.'

The councillor, feeling relieved at having got that off his chest, made a swift exit.

A week later, a notice appeared in *The Evesbury Echo*. The announcement went as follows:

PUBLIC MEETING

TO DISCUSS A PROPOSED HOUSING DEVELOPMENT ON THE MEADOW, GENTLY VILLAGE.

EVESBURY COMMUNITY HALL

7.30 PM ON THURSDAY, 27TH SEPTEMBER

DOORS OPEN 7.00

'Are you going?' Archie enquired.

'Try and stop me,' said Ruby.

20

On the morning of the meeting, a letter arrived at the cottage and Ruby wasted no time in opening it.

'Well?' said Archie, observing the puzzled frown on her face.

'It's the mayor,' said Ruby.

'One of Maisie's mares?'

'What? No, the sort with two legs.'

'His worship, the mayor?'

'Exactly. Sir Stanley Allen, or is it Sir Allen Stanley? I can never remember.'

'Hasn't he signed it?'

'Yes, but it's just a squiggle.'

'What's he got in mind?'

'He says he's anxious to discuss the dispute over The Meadow housing proposal before the meeting and would I please come to his office and to bring my nephew.'

'Why does he want me?'

'He doesn't say. He says he'll send a car to pick us up at six this evening and we can have a lift to the meeting afterwards.'

'I smell a rat.'

'So do I. But he assures me it's a genuine attempt to solve the dispute over The Meadow and he will send the mayoral car to pick us up, complete with chauffeur.'

'I see. Will you recognise the mayoral car?'

'It has the coat of arms painted on the side.'

'Could I see the letter?'

'Of course.' She handed it over.

Archie gave it a quick scan. 'Headed notepaper. It looks genuine enough.'

'So, what do we do?'

'Where exactly is the mayoral office?'

'It's in the council building. Pilbeam House.'

Archie pondered. 'Have we anything to gain by going?'

'I don't know. Maybe he's trying to decide which side to support. It would be good to have the mayor on our side.'

'Okay, if car and driver look genuine, we'll give it a go.'

When they heard the car arrive, Archie went out to do a quick check. At the gate, the driver was standing by the ancient limousine, wearing a chauffeur's dark suit and peaked cap. He had the patient air of a man whose work entailed long periods of waiting. 'Good afternoon, sir,' he said pleasantly

'It certainly is,' said Archie. 'And you are?'

'Neville,' sir.

'Right, Neville. You don't mind if I ask a few questions do you?'

'By all means.'

'Okay. How long have you worked for the mayor?'

'Oh, about four years I think, on and off.'

'On and off?'

'Yes. I'm not employed solely by the mayor. I belong to a hire firm who supply drivers to various people. I drive for many other people as well.'

'I see. And what about the car?'

'The car?'

'Is it also hired?'

'No sir, it belongs to the council. Only the driver is hired.'

'Would you mind if I took a look at your driving licence?'

'Not at all sir.' Neville obligingly fished out his licence and handed it over.

Archie scrutinised the document, nodded his approval and handed it back.

'Okay. So, how do you find the mayor?'

'I beg your pardon, sir.'

'What sort of bloke is he?'

'It's really not my place to comment on clients.'

'I'm pleased to hear it. So what, exactly are your orders for today?'

'To pick you up at 6 p.m., take you to the Mayor's office for a meeting and then return in time to drive you to the community hall for the half past seven public meeting.'

'Excellent, you've passed the test.'

'The test, sir?'

'The credibility test. We thought this whole thing might be a hoax, but you seem to be the real thing. I'll just fetch my aunt and we can be on our way.'

When they arrived, Pilbeam House was a fading image in the twilight. No lights were visible and a white van marked EVES-BURY ELECTRICAL stood outside. The front door was open revealing a dark interior.

'Know what's going on, Neville?' Archie asked.

'I believe one of the circuits has blown. Lights are affected in some parts of the building but not others. Apparently rats have nibbled through some of the wiring.'

'I see. Not surprising I suppose, considering the number inhabiting the place.'

'Let's just go in,' said Ruby. 'So you'll pick us up in about an hour, Neville?'

'That is so, madam.'

'Right, we'll see you later then.' She climbed out of the car and headed for the front door.

'To hear is to obey,' said Archie as he got out and followed her.

Inside the hall, the darkness was relieved by a subdued light coming from the half-open door of a side room.

'Hello!' called Archie.

Seconds later, the light moved into the hall closely followed by a shadowy figure holding a hand lamp that dazzled them, 'Good evening,' said a gruff voice. 'The mayor apologies for the inconvenience but he's been forced to change offices to a room where the lights are working. Please follow me.'

Without further ado, the ghostly figure took off, along a corridor and down some steps. Half blinded, they followed, until they came to a door. Their escort opened it and beckoned them in. They walked through and found themselves in a brightly lit room that appeared empty. 'Sorry about all this,' said their escort, but I'll see you later.' With that, the door slammed shut with a clang. Archie was quick to turn and grab the handle but it was already locked. 'Hey!' he shouted, banging on the door with his fist. But all they heard was the sound of retreating footsteps.

Ruby heaved a sigh. 'Another fine mess,' she said.

In the corridor, Sidney Burke was congratulating himself on having pulled off an amazing feat. The carefully forged letter, followed by use of the mayoral chauffeur and finally, his brilliant role-playing that had lured them into the cellar. Admittedly, Charlie Leggit had played a small part in persuading an electrician to fake the blackout in parts of the building, but he was the one who had made the whole thing work. Joe Bradley would have to apologise to him after this. He returned to his office in high spirits.

Inside the room, Archie wondered aloud who their captor might be. 'He may have been just a shadow, but he had a familiar walk, don't you think Aunt Ruby?'

'He certainly did,' she said. 'It was that bogus building inspector all over again.'

At that moment, the overhead light went out and a dim emergency light came on.

21

In the Evesbury Community Hall, Mildred Crouch, the vicar's wife, was getting anxious. The number of locals gathered there was well below expectations and worse still, Ruby was nowhere to be seen. The opposition however, had gathered in numbers. Joe Bradley was there, apparently with most of his workforce while Councillor Leggit was in the chair. It appeared that the voice of democracy was about to be drowned out.

An out-of-breath Maisie came into the hall. 'It's no use,' she said. 'I've been knocking on doors but they all said the same thing. A note was pushed through their letterbox this afternoon, informing them that the meeting was cancelled. I assured them it was still on and some said they would come but a lot were either out or had made other arrangements.'

'A note through the door?' Mrs Crouch looked baffled. 'Who on earth would do that?'

'It looks like another dirty trick.'

'But what about Ruby and Archibald? Do you think they've had the same note?'

'Ruby wouldn't take any notice of a note pushed through the door. I think she's been diverted somehow. I don't know what we can do now.'

'Perhaps we should pray,' said the vicar's wife.

In the cellar, two pairs of eyes were becoming accustomed to the gloom. The emergency light was just sufficient to show they were in a coal cellar. There was a heap of the stuff in the middle of the room and in one corner stood a rather ancient-looking boiler. It emitted a faint glow and made occasional gurgling sounds as it pushed water around the system.

'Well, at least we can keep warm,' said Archie. 'And if somebody comes down to put more coal on, I could always hit him with the fire shovel.'

'Archibald! You'll do no such thing!' Ruby said. 'I don't want you arrested for GBH. Besides, they've done this just to keep us from the meeting. That means we'll be let out when it's over.'

'Yeah, I suppose you're right,' said Archie gloomily. 'What an idiot to fall for such a trick. Anyway, let's at least look at the possibility of getting out of here.'

Their inspection of the place was not encouraging. They were surrounded by dust-blackened brick walls, in one of which was a stout-looking door. Archie tried to open it but it refused to budge. He put his shoulder to it and gave a heave. It seemed to yield slightly and after a harder shove, it gave way and he was catapulted into the space beyond.

Ruby gave a faint shriek. 'Are you all right?' she enquired anxiously as she helped him up off the floor.'

'Only a mild dislocation,' said Archie, rubbing his shoulder. 'So where are we now?'

They looked round. It was darker and seemed smaller than the boiler room. They felt their way carefully around. There were no doors but in one corner Archie kicked against a clutter of tinny sounding objects. Taking one of these back into the light, he discovered it was a half-empty tin of paint.

'Now you know,' said Ruby. 'This is where the decorators hide their stuff.'

'Yep, you're right.' He suddenly looked thoughtful. 'I wonder?' he muttered, stepping back into the darkness.

'Wonder what?'

'Whether they've left a step ladder here.'

'A step ladder. What good will that do?'

'Hang on and I'll show you.'

There was more clattering and scraping and he appeared suddenly, wrestling with something big and awkward-looking. 'Bingo!' he said, triumphantly, propping them against the wall.

Ruby stared at him. 'And just what good will they do us, do you think, nephew?'

'Just depends on whether they'll reach or not, Aunt. If they do, they may be our means of escape.'

'I don't follow.'

'Well, look at that heap of coal. Where do you think it came from?'

'A coal mine?'

'Full marks for knowing that, but I meant just before it arrived on the floor here.'

'Through a manhole I suppose. That's how most coal cellars work.'

'Exactly! And this ladder could give me access to it.'

She looked at the coal heap and then at the roof. 'Isn't that risky?'

'Very risky as things are. But if we clear some of the coal away and stand the steps on the floor, it might be possible to reach the manhole. Let's have a go!'

Archie picked up the shovel and set to work. Ruby took hold of some of the bigger lumps and threw them aside. It proved to be a hard and dirty job, covering them in black dust and leaving them panting and sweating. Finally, they'd cleared enough of the floor to set up the steps.

'I hope this is all worth it,' said Ruby, leaning against the wall.

'It will be if it gets us out of here.'

'Count me out. I'm no good at heights.'

'Okay,' said Archie as he climbed the steps. 'I'll find you another way.'

'Just be careful, Archie.'

'Caution is my middle name,' he said, as the noise of a heavy manhole cover being displaced rumbled round the room. The last Ruby saw of him was a pair of trouser legs disappearing through the hole in the roof.

In the Community Hall, Councillor Leggit was winding up his address. He beamed at the audience. 'Well I think we've had a very good discussion,' he said, 'and everyone has had a chance to express their views.'

'Rubbish!' Mrs Crouch was on her feet. 'What about all the people who received false cancellation notices? They didn't get the chance to express their views. This is a disgrace!'

'I'm sorry madam, but I haven't an idea what you're talking about.'

'I've already told you. This afternoon, cancellation notices were posted through people's doors.' She looked round the hall. 'If anyone here had a hand in posting those notices, would they like to tell us about it?'

There was a silence. no one, it seemed, was ready to confess.

'I'm sorry,' said Councillor Leggit, 'it seems no one here can help you. And now I think it's time we had the vote.'

'The vote!' Maisie and Mrs Crouch cried in unison. 'Who said anything about a vote?' Mrs Crouch asked.

Councillor Leggit treated her to an oily smile. 'Dear lady, how else can we test opinion? Whitehall have asked us to test local feeling before they make a ruling. A vote is the only way.'

'First,' said Mrs Crouch, 'I am not your "dear lady" and second any vote here today would be rigged.'

'Really?' Councillor Leggit assumed his surprised look which he reserved for occasions such as this. 'Well that is a matter for investigation. I will see it is looked into.'

'Good,' said Mrs Crouch. 'So this meeting will be postponed then?'

'I'm afraid not. You see, these meetings can be costly. There's the publicity, hire of the hall and so on and I would not be able to justify it.'

'This is outrageous!' Mrs Crouch cried. 'An affront to democracy.'

'I'm sorry. The Accounts Committee would never sanction another meeting. We must vote now.'

22

Sidney Burke was comfortably settled in the small office in Pilbeam House and feeling rather pleased with himself. He'd carried out his instructions to the letter, luring that pair into the cellar, cancelling their ride in the mayoral limousine to attend a meeting, and the only remaining task was to let them out later when the meeting would be over. Meanwhile, to pass the time, he was engrossed in one of his comic books.

The bit he was reading involved one of his favourite characters, the intrepid adventurer, Sledgehammer Smith. In this episode Smith (who'd earned the nickname 'sledgehammer' because of the power of his left hook as an amateur boxer) was embarking on yet another dangerous mission. This one was set in desert country. He'd entered the palace of Sheik-y-Bhuti, the cruel slave master, in order to rescue a girl recently abducted from among a group of European archaeologists. At this very moment, Smith was creeping across the palace's marbled hall, when he was suddenly confronted by a figure stepping out of nowhere. It was the sheik's personal bodyguard, a huge black Nubian wielding an enormous curved sword. The guard advanced on him with glittering eyes.

Sidney was enthralled. His hair was practically standing on end as he paused in a fever of excitement. At this point, a small sound caused him to look up. Before him stood a black figure with (it seemed to him) glittering eyes. He appeared to be carrying a pencil and a sheet of paper. Sidney let out a startled yelp.

'Sorry to trouble you mate,' said the figure. 'I've just delivered a ton of best cobbles and I need a signature.'

'You know you nearly gave me a heart attack?'

'Sorry mate, but you are the only one around. It's just a matter of you checking that I've delivered that coal.'

'I'm busy right now. Anyway, coal deliveries are not my responsibility.'

'I see. Will it be your responsibility when they find a body down there?'

'A body? What are you talking about?'

'Well, I was tipping stuff into the cellar when I heard a voice shouting for help. I shouted back but there was no answer. Someone may be lying there unconscious, or even worse.'

Sidney scrambled to his feet. 'Stay there!' he ordered as he grabbed the lamp and rushed out of the room.

'Good luck, mate,' muttered Archie, 'mind how you go.'

In the cellar, Ruby heard steps approaching. Whoever it was seemed to be in a hurry. Then a key turned in the lock and the door was flung open. Sidney looked round. 'Where is he?' he said.

'Where's who?'

'The bloke who was with you, of course, who else?'

'Oh, him. He's in there,' she said, pointing to the small cellar.

Sidney dashed through the door. In the small room, he directed the light round the walls and into the corners. Nothing. He tried again. Still nothing. When he emerged, he didn't seem best pleased. 'There's no one there,' he said. 'I must ... His voice trailed away when he realised he was talking to an empty room. Worse still, the door was locked.

In the grounds of Pilbeam House, two blackened figures found each other. 'Have we time to get to that meeting?' Ruby asked.

'Yes, plenty of time,' Archie assured her. 'We can walk.'

'But I can't go like this. I need to get cleaned up first.'

'Ah! that may be difficult.' He thought a moment. 'Tell you what, you can use Maisie's flat. It's on the way.'

'Maisie will be out. She'll have gone to the meeting.'

'I know, but she won't mind us using it. Er, I do have a key.'

'Do you indeed?' said Ruby, giving him an inscrutable look.

'I don't think there's time for both of us to clean up. I'll have to go as I am.'

'That'll be a treat for Maisie,' said Ruby.

23

In the Community Centre, Mrs Crouch had decided there was only one course of action to stop the way the meeting was being manoeuvred. She explained it to the group.

'A what?' Maisie enquired.

'A filibuster,' Mrs Crouch explained, 'means we use up time by endless talking. 'It's a tried and trusted tactic,' she assured them. 'In parliament for example, I believe it's been used to talk out an unpopular bill.'

'That's all very well,' Maisie objected, 'but they are professional windbags. What are we going to talk about?'

'Anything you like, dear,' said Mrs Crouch, 'so long as it uses up the time.'

Some time later, Maisie had done her bit. It proved to be very popular, consisting as it did of talking about the romantic experiences of her life. Now, her voice had reached the croaky stage and she could no longer carry on, she'd handed over the reins to

Mrs Crouch, the vicar's wife.

Of course none of what Maisie said had any relevance to the matter in hand, but no one seemed to care except for two people. Councillor Leggit, who made several futile efforts to interrupt, and Joe Bradley, who was displaying symptoms of apoplexy.

Into this scene, Ruby made her entrance. She glanced round before slipping in to a seat at the back. Maisie was delighted to see her.

'Ruby, how lovely!' she said in a hoarse whisper. 'We thought you weren't going to turn up. What happened?'

'Tell you later,' Ruby whispered back.

'You're looking very smart in that white mac. I've got one exactly like it at home.'

Ruby blushed slightly. 'I know, but it's not there now.'

'Why not?'

'I'm wearing it.'

Maisie gaped, lost for words.

'Archibald will be here shortly,' said Ruby. 'His appearance is a bit different too.'

Mrs Crouch was still spouting, but she was struggling. The audience didn't seem to appreciate her in the same way they had enjoyed Maisie's reminiscences. Their previous enthusiasm had evaporated and one or two had dozed off.

'And as it says in the Book of Common Prayer,' Mrs Crouch droned on, 'be of one mind in *an* house.'

'An house? shouted a voice. 'Well hurry it up. I have *an* home to go to.'

There was a general murmur of agreement. Charlie Leggit seized his chance. Getting to his feet he said, 'Well thank you so much for that contribution, dear lady.' It really is getting late and we must wrap this up.' There were shouts of agreement and the vicar's wife, realising that the mood had turned hostile, sat down.

At this point, Archie slid in through the door and moved to a seat near Ruby. 'How's it going?' he whispered.

'Not well,' said Ruby. 'He's going to call a vote and we're outnumbered.'

Maisie, meanwhile, was regarding his black figure with astonishment. 'Is that you, Archie?' she said.

'I'm afraid it is. I'll explain later.'

'I'll be all ears.'

Councillor Leggit had noted the entry of the dark figure and was immediately intrigued. He watched as the man moved to join the ranks of the opposition and decided to find out more. He cleared his throat. 'Excuse me sir,' he said, 'are you in the right place?'

Archie looked round to see who the councillor could be addressing. Seeing no other male personages in the vicinity he said, 'Are you talking to me?'

'I am indeed, sir,' the councillor said importantly. 'Of course, this is a public meeting and all are welcome but I was wondering if it was your intention to vote this evening?'

'It certainly is.' said Archie, 'do you have any objections to that?'

'Actually, yes I'm afraid I do. You see the vote will be confined to *bona fide* residents of the area, not holiday makers, temporary residents, drifters or visitors from overseas.'

'I see,' said Archie. So does that rule out the workers brought along by Mr Bradley?'

'Not at all. They live in the area, so they qualify.'

'Really?' Archie gave the builder's group a searching look. 'As

I understand it, many of them are here only temporarily. Why don't you check to make find out how many really are *bona fide* residents?'

There was an immediate buzz in the hall. Charlie Leggit puffed out his cheeks and wondered how to respond while Joe Bradley gave him an incendiary sort of glare.

'Very well,' the councillor said finally. 'I will check. He leant down from the platform and addressed a man in the front row.

'Are you *bona fide*?' he asked.

'No, mate. I'm Church of England.'

The councillor decided it was time to change tack. He looked across the group and said, 'Gentlemen, if any of you are *not* a *bona fide* member of this community, would you please raise your hand.' No one stirred.

'Well I think that's pretty conclusive!' the councillor said, looking smugly towards Archie. 'I think it's time to stop talking and get to the important part of the proceedings. It's time to take a vote. The issue is, may I remind you, about whether we need more housing in the area or not. There is a proposal on the table to build houses on The Meadow in the nearby village of Gently, and you should vote either in favour or against. It is not a binding vote. It will not oblige the council to do one thing or the other but it will send a very strong signal both to the local council and to central government regarding the democratic wishes of the local people. I want you ...'

'For god's sake, get on with it!' Joe Bradley was feeling the strain of having to talk out of the side of his mouth rather than bawling down the councillor's ear.

The councillor himself would have preferred to go on for much longer. He loved the sound of his own voice, especially in meetings, but he supposed it would be wise not to aggravate the builder any further. He noted with satisfaction that the black chap had disappeared, no doubt realising it was a lost cause.

'Could I have your attention, please ladies and gentlemen,' he called. Will those in favour of ...'

At that point the sudden ear-splitting sound of an electric bell rang through the hall and at the same time a voice from the direction of the entrance lobby bawled 'FIRE!'

There was a moment of frozen silence before someone in the audience said, 'That's it! Let's get out of here!'

The reaction was immediate and after a brief thunder of boots on the wood floor, only Leggit and a red-faced Bradley remained on the platform.

Ruby stood up. 'Right Mr Chairman,' she said sweetly, 'Can we get on with the vote now? Just remember that your position does not allow you yourself to vote. We may just have time before the fire takes hold.'

The councillor looked round and realised that he and Bradley were well outnumbered.

'I don't think so,' he said. 'We must evacuate the building immediately.' Not waiting to check if others were leaving, he made a bee line for the door at a speed he'd not achieved since Ruby waved a shotgun at him.

'Perhaps we'd better make a move too,' said Maisie.

'There's no rush,' said Ruby. 'Let's just wait for Archibald to turn that bell off.'

24

Joe Bradley's patience was wearing thin after the events of the last few days. It seemed to him that Councillor Leggit was more of a hindrance than a help. Leggit was the one who had persuaded him to buy that field in the first place, with promises that permission to build would be a mere formality. Now, weeks later, he was no further forward. That abortive meeting yesterday had been the last straw. The councillor had allowed himself to be out-manoeuvred by a vicar's wife, a barmaid and that old biddy from the cottage. It seemed they'd conspired to delay things long enough to allow some idiot to sabotage the proceedings by setting off the fire alarm when there was no fire.

As the builder brooded on all this, one thing became clear. From now on he would not be listening to any advice other than his own. Already a plan was forming in his mind. It was not something that would get him and his gang to the starting line, but it would, however, be a signal to all concerned that Joe Bradley would not be thwarted, and opposition to this scheme would only delay the inevitable.

In Gently Village Hall, another meeting of the Ladies Club was in progress. The visiting speaker, Mrs Dora Watchett, was in full flow. As always, Dora was enthusiastic about her subject, which was basically herself in some remote location. This time it was Patagonia.

She had quite an extensive set of colour slides. These consisted of Dora with local families, Dora with children, Dora with the tribal chief, Dora with a flock of sheep, and so on. As the slides clicked their way monotonously through the projector, more and more of the audience were falling victim to the soporific atmosphere. Mrs Crouch, the vicar's wife, who was in charge of the event, was listening anxiously for the first signs of a snore. If one did break out, then she was ready to pounce on the offender with a prod in the ribs.

It was Sally Tucker, daughter of the village postmistress, who brought about a change in proceedings. She entered the room quietly and peered around the audience. Spotting her mother, she went quickly across and tapped her on the shoulder. Mrs Tucker woke with a start. 'Very interesting,' she mumbled. 'Is it time for refreshments?'

'Mum!' said Sally urgently, 'you must come. Mr Bradley's started work!'

'What?'

'The builders are on The Meadow and they've started work!'

By this time, half the sleepers were awake and a sudden babble soon woke the others. Mrs Crouch took immediate control. 'Could you tell us a bit more Sally,' she said. 'How have they started work?'

'Well, they're digging holes.'

'Digging holes!?' Ruby was on her feet. 'You mean holes for foundations?'

'Er, I dunno. Just holes.'

The news catapulted Ruby out of her chair and brought the meeting out of its stupor. Everyone started talking at once. Ruby demanded to know more, Mrs Tucker fretted that her shop had been left unattended and the guest speaker made frantic appeals for a little more time so that she could finish her lecture.

Above the din, Mrs Crouch's voice went *fortissimo*. 'Hold on, ladies,' she commanded, 'this concerns all of us, so we'll go

down to The Meadow together! Let us show a united front!'
There was a general murmur of agreement.

'Better still, let's make it a proper demo,' said Maisie.

'How do you mean, a proper demo?'

'Placards with messages on them. We've done it before.'

'I don't think we've time for all that,' Ruby said grimly. 'The sooner we get there the better!'

'Don't worry, it won't take long,' said Maisie. 'There are some old placards and spare sheets of paper in the storeroom. Left over from that demo we had about cuts to the local bus service,' she explained.

'Good idea, Maisie,' said Mrs Crouch. 'A few strong words should get the message across. And while you're doing that, I'll ask *The Echo* to send someone along and also talk to Mr Whittle, the scoutmaster. The troop are in the church hall right now and they can escort us to the site.'

'Right!' said Maisie. 'Let's go!'

'Hold on a moment!' It was their guest speaker. 'I've only a few slides left. It won't take long to show them and if I could just ...'

But the rest of the sentence was lost in what sounded like the noise of a mass jail break.

On The Meadow, Joe Bradley was in a much better mood. Showbiz, he decided, had nothing on him. He thrived on the smell of the gloss paint and the roar of the cement mixer. So here he was, showing that he was someone who got on with things instead of endlessly talking. He sat in the cab of his lorry, watching measurements being taken, levels surveyed, holes dug and string lines set out.

Of course, he knew very well that he couldn't actually start building. That would be to risk having to tear it all down again. What he was banking on, was that the locals would see he meant business and issues like planning permission were mere hiccups on the way. If he got that message across it should discourage any further attempts at sabotage.

Outside the village hall, the procession formed up at the kerbside. The Gently Scout Group was at the front while the ladies fell in behind. At the head was the scoutmaster, Arnold Whittle, a local solicitor whose passions were scouting and the environment. This protest seemed to him to be a perfect exercise for his little troop.

Now he stood, eyeing the procession and waiting for its constituent parts to settle down. When he was satisfied, he called, 'Are we all ready?'

The group mumbled assent.

'Does that include you, Donald?'

'Yessir,' said a beefy lad with a big drum strapped to his front.

'Very good then. Forward March!'

At this, Donald banged hard on his big drum, deafening his immediate neighbours and causing a flock of birds to take off from a nearby tree. After a few bars from the big drum, the other drummers joined in, while the buglers blew a discordant blast on their bugles. So they set off, marching raggedly but in high spirits.

A short time later, the sound of the band floated in on the breeze to reach the ears of the toiling builders. One by one, they stopped work as the sounds grew louder. Joe Bradley, noticing that something was up, stepped down from his lorry and joined the listeners. 'What the hell's that?' he asked.

'Dunno, boss. A band of some sort innit?'

'Yeah, and it ain't the BBC symphony orchestra!' said someone else.

25

The sound of the band grew gradually louder until, round the bend in the lane, they marched into view. The builders stared open mouthed at the strange sight of a middle-aged man in shorts, knobbly knees exposed, leading a group of small boys making discordant noises on drums and bugles. Behind them came a group of determined looking ladies, waving banners with messages that were not yet within reading distance. Judging by the general air of menace surrounding the approaching army, they were not messages of peace and goodwill.

Joe Bradley scowled and muttered to himself. This was exactly the sort of thing he was trying to prevent. Out loud he said, 'Right, you lot, just get on with what you're doing. I'll see to this.' With that, he stood with arms folded, like a general contemplating his next move on the field of battle.

The messages were soon within reading distance and they spelled out the mood of the marchers ranging from a mild NO HOUSES HERE and KEEP THE MEADOW GREEN to a more robust HANDS OFF OUR LAND and SHOVE OFF BRADLEY. There had been some attempts at something stronger, but all such messages had been vetoed by Mrs Crouch on the grounds of maintaining public decency. The parade arrived at the field in good order and came to a halt at its edge.

A strange calm settled over the scene as the two sides stood facing each other, separated by no more than the length of a cricket pitch. The scout band fell silent, the ladies stared at the builders and the builders stared back. The stand-off was ended when Mrs Crouch suddenly spoke up in her most commanding voice.

'Why don't you all go home?' she said. 'All except Mr Bradley, that is. We'd like a word with him.'

Bradley's face reddened. 'Stay right where you are,' he bellowed. 'You take orders from me and nobody else.' Then, turning to the watching ladies he said, 'And you lot, don't take another step or you'll be trespassing. This is my land.'

'Mr Bradley,' said Mrs Crouch, politely, 'people don't care for the way all this has been handled. The Meadow has always been a part of local life for use as a place of recreation and rest. We need to talk about it.'

The word 'talk' seemed to upset the builder further. 'Talk?' he snarled. 'Don't talk to me about talk. There's been little else. Go away and talk amongst yourselves if you want but just leave me out of it.'

Ruby, who had been standing silently fuming at all this, was suddenly galvanised into action, 'He's right, Mildred,' she called. 'Never mind the talk, let's get some action!' With that, she set off towards Bradley, waving her banner. Mrs Crouch, alarmed by this sudden change of plan, took off after her with a cry of 'Stop, Ruby please!' As Bradley watched them charging towards him, he picked up a spade and prepared to ward them off.

Meanwhile a couple arrived from *The Echo*, one equipped with a camera. 'Wow! Looks like the Charge of the Light Brigade,' said the photographer. 'I'll get some pictures.'

Ruby's headlong dash slowed a little as she closed the gap and Mrs Crouch caught up with her. 'Ruby!' she gasped. 'Ruby please don't ...' she was cut short as her right foot got tangled in one of the many string lines criss-crossing the field. She fell forward, still clutching the banner. Her arms went out to save herself and the banner, bearing the legend WE SHALL NOT BE MOVED, shot forward and caught Bradley squarely on the chin. He went down like a pole-axed steer and stayed down.

Ruby came to an immediate halt. 'Are you all right?' she asked in sudden concern as she held out a helping hand.

The heap on the floor untangled itself and accepted the help. 'Yes, I'm all right,' said Mrs Crouch as she got to her feet, 'but what about poor Mr Bradley?'

'Oh, him!' said Ruby scornfully. 'You got him fair and square Mildred, I couldn't have done better myself!'

'But we'll have to help him. I think I may have knocked him out.'

'Good, that should keep him quiet for a while.'

Mrs Crouch stared worriedly at the builder before eyeing the crowd of rather sheepish-looking builders. 'Will somebody give him a hand please. You need to get him to the hospital.'

There was no great rush to comply until two at the front of the crowd, wilting under Mrs Crouch's commanding look, came forward to pick up the body. They managed to lift it into the cab of the lorry before one of them climbed into the driver's seat and the vehicle took off in the direction of the town.

Without their leader, the builders shuffled about, uncertain what to do next. 'Er, right then,' one of them said, 'I think we ought to go.'

'By all means,' said Mrs Crouch, 'just as soon as you've tidied up.'

'Tidied up?'

'Yes,' said Ruby. 'You've made a mess of this field. The least you can do is clear it all away. You can get rid of the pegs, fill in any holes, put the turf back where it belongs, take your equipment and clear off.'

'But we've only just finished the work.'

'Then you'd better unfinish it, unless you want to be prosecuted for breaching the regulations.'

'What regulations?'

'The Building Regulations of course.'

'We're just doing what we're told.'

'Would you rather I informed the police?'

One or two looked extremely uncomfortable at this suggestion. 'Betta gerron with it then,' one of them said.

'I can't be doing with this,' said another. 'I'm going home.' With that, he marched off, looking less than pleased. Then one of the builders picked up a loose turf and threw it aside in frustration. Unfortunately, it struck one of the ladies and a moment later, there was a general melee as others started throwing things.

The reporter rubbed her hands together. 'Looks like we've a good story this week,' she said to the photographer. 'This should please the editor.'

Maisie, in the thick of it, picked a piece of loose turf and threw it at the head of a woolly-hatted individual with his back towards her.

'Take that!' she shouted as the woolly hat staggered sideways.

Recovering his balance, he turned round. Maisie's jaw dropped as she beheld a swarthy featured, rather good looking young man. 'Why you do that?' he demanded.

'I'm so sorry,' she said. 'I was aiming at someone else.'

'I think I'll quit,' he said. 'I only come here to work. Nobody tol' me you 'ave to fight first.'

'Oh, it's nothing to worry about,' said Maisie. 'Tell me, where are you from?'

'Valencia.'

'Wow!' she said. 'You've no idea how romantic that sounds. What did you do there?'

'I am a student,' he said.

'Of what?'

'Eh?'

'What are you a student of? What are you studying?'

'Ah, *si*! I study European history. That is why I am here. To see some of your historic places but I also have to work for my living.'

'That's lucky!' said Maisie. 'The place I work in has a long history. You should come and take a look around.'

'You work in a stately home?'

'No, it's a pub actually.'

'A pub?'

'Yes, very old. Said to be haunted by Dick Turpin.'

'Dick who?'

'Never mind. Why don't you come this evening when I'll be there? It's called The Highwayman.'

'Will I see this Dick Turnip?'

'Turpin. Well I've never seen him and to be honest I think it's a load of codswallop. Still, it brings the punters in. And we do have a range of drinks and a friendly atmosphere. You'd enjoy it.'

He appeared baffled by some of this information but said 'Okay, maybe. Do you know what is going on here?'

'This?' She waved an arm airily at the surrounding mayhem. 'A slight difference of opinion, that's all. The demo is a good old British tradition. It's quite friendly really,' she said as a clod of earth struck her on the shoulder. 'But never mind this. I'm Maisie, how about you?'

'My name is Carlos and I am very pleased to meet you,' he said with a bow.

'I'm pleased to meet you Carlos. Tell me a bit about yourself.'

'Maybe later. For now I'd rather get away.'

'Of course. Cutting through the trees over there brings you to the main road. And don't forget what I said. Call in and see us.'

'I look forward to it.' He bowed, took her hand and pressed it to his lips.

At that moment a tubby chap puffed past, pursued by Ruby waving the remains of a splintered banner. 'Fraternising with the enemy are we?' she snarled at Maisie. 'I'll see you later.'

'You'd better go Carlos,' giggled Maisie, 'before they lynch me.'

'Of course ... *Adios!*' With that he waved and took off towards the trees. Maisie sighed and wondered, not for the first time, if it was possible to be in love with two people at the same time.

In another part of the field, Mrs Proctor, a farmer's wife, was arguing with a small, wiry chap in a hard hat. Like Ruby, she had lost the top off her banner and had the remains of the pole over her shoulder like a soldier on parade. The fact that he was holding a spade seemed to have upset her.

'Why are you digging up our village?' she asked.

'I'm just doing my job.'

'Well, why don't you go and do it somewhere else?'

'Because this is where I've been told to do it.'

'Well, this is our village and we don't want you.'

'I didn't choose it. Anyway, we're helping to keep the place going. Spending our money here.'

'Oh, yes?' She peered at him. 'Haven't I seen you in my farm shop?'

'Very likely. That proves my point. I'm putting money in your pocket.'

'Well we can manage without you so you can take your custom

elsewhere.'

'Maybe I should. The last cabbage I bought from you had a caterpillar in it.'

'Did it? Well, we don't charge extra for the protein.'

'And your potatoes had a lot of soil on them.'

'There's a reason for that.'

'What's that then?'

'We grow them in the ground.'

'Well, you should wash them.'

'There are some washed ones in the shop. You just have to look.'

'They cost more.'

'Well, what do you expect? I suppose you'd like free delivery as well?'

'That's the best suggestion you've made yet.'

'Could I make another one?'

'Please do.'

'Why don't you try the village chemist for his headache pills? They're very good.'

'I haven't got a headache.'

'Just be patient,' said Mrs Proctor, raising her shortened pole with both hands and bringing it down on his hard hat with a crash. He staggered sideways and stood for a moment on sagging knees. Then, apparently deciding that enough was enough, he tottered away to be lost in the crowd. Mrs Proctor looked round, ready for more action while her blood was up. However, the battle was gradually ebbing as more of the building gang decided that this wasn't what they were getting paid for and made off to look for places of safety. They were followed by loud jeers. Most of the scouts were looking disappointed at being kept out of the fray, but made up for it by giving the fleeing mob a noisy send-off.

Meanwhile, the reporter was still frantically scribbling.

119

26

In the offices of *The Echo,* the editor worried about the latest edition of the weekly paper. True, he had an eye-witness account of the skirmish on The Meadow and true, it was more interesting than the usual local stuff, but he knew it wasn't enough. The reason it wasn't enough was that the paper's owner, Sir Roscoe Hornby, was on the warpath. The editor went over in his mind the events of the previous day when the tycoon had paid him a visit with the express purpose of voicing his displeasure at the paper's fading popularity.

Puffing on a fat cigar, Sir Roscoe had lambasted the editor on the grounds that the paper was boring. 'Do you get that?' he'd bawled in an explosion of hyperbole and cigar ash, 'BORING!' As a result, circulation was down, advertising revenue was down and, surprise, surprise, profits were down. At the end of this broadside, the Ed was left in no doubt that he had either to shape up or ship out.

The episode had kept the Ed awake for half the night as he wrestled with the problem of what to do next. Sir Roscoe had been unequivocal. It was, he stated loudly, HUMAN INTEREST that sold newspapers. The editor had protested that that was what *The Echo* was all about. Human Interest, he said, dripped from its pages. There were articles covering sport, books, theatre, health, and so on and if those weren't human interest stories, he didn't know what was. There was also Mrs Gimlett's regular feature on cookery and Billy Todd's DIY page which only this week carried step-by-step instructions on how to turn your old trouser press into an ironing board. In fact, the editor claimed, it was human interest all the way, and if Sir Roscoe would just ...

But Sir Roscoe interrupted to make it clear that *he* would not be just doing anything. 'This meeting,' he said, 'is about *your* incompetence, not mine. So let me ask you this,' he continued. 'Suppose you were to ask your cookery writer how to make a boring dish more appealing,' he said, 'what do you think she would suggest?'

The editor considered this. 'I dunno. Maybe add some brown sauce?'

'Brown sauce!' thundered the tycoon. 'Are you trying to be funny?'

The Ed assured him that trying to be funny was the last thing on his mind.

'No,' said the tycoon, 'what she would probably do is to recommend spicing it up. There are all sorts of exotic things you can include in dishes to make them more exciting. Have you got that?'

The editor took a minute to absorb this. 'Spice it up?' he said. 'Do you want me to have a word with Mrs Gimlett? Get her to ease off on the steak and kidney pie recipes in favour of more curry?'

Sir Roscoe nearly choked on his cigar. He had no wish to interfere with Mrs Gimlett's recipes in any way, shape or form, he said. What he was doing was giving the editor an example of how adding certain ingredients could make the whole thing more interesting.

'It's an ANALOGY,' he bawled.

The editor thought this over and was suddenly appalled. 'By suggesting that the paper should be spiced up, do you mean to turn it into some sort of *scandal* sheet?'

The tycoon appeared to have simmered down a touch. 'There's no need to shout,' he said. 'I think you understand the sort of human interest I want, so I'll leave you to it.' With that he departed, leaving the office wreathed in cigar smoke and editorial gloom.

After this pasting and a sleepless night, the editor was now faced with a decision. Scandal or the sack seemed to be the only two options available to him. Gloomily he went over the report of the confrontation on The Meadow. Flipping through the file, he came across a photograph that gave him food for thought. He would not normally publish anything so controversial, but it was his neck on the block. He decided there and then to do a rewrite.

It was early morning at the vicarage and Mrs Crouch, the vicar's wife, was intent on giving her husband, Bernard, a good start to the day. She had already eaten and was on her way from the kitchen with his breakfast tray when newspapers popped through the letterbox in the hall. She collected them and went into the dining room.

'There we are, dear,' she said, as she deposited the tray on the table, 'Enjoy your breakfast and a read. You've got two papers this morning, The usual daily and the *The Evesbury Echo*. Anyway, I'm out this morning. There's a meeting of the hospital fund-raising committee and I need to do a bit of shopping. And while I'm out, I'll check on the builder who got injured yesterday to make sure he's all right. Anyway, I'll leave you in peace while I just pop upstairs to get ready. Bye dear,' she said, giving him a peck on the cheek. 'I'll see you later.' With that, she bustled out, leaving the still sleepy vicar to mumble his thanks and turn his attention to the contents of the tray.

For the vicar, the early morning transition from sleep to a state of full alertness was always a slow process. After rising from his bed, bathing and dressing at a leisurely pace, he would descend to the dining room to partake of a reviving cup of tea followed by eggs, toast and a stroll through the paper.

As he munched his way through the menu he scanned the two papers for the important stuff first. It was while he was pouring his second cup of tea that his attention was arrested by the pictures on the front of *The Echo*. There were scenes of a dispute on The Meadow. One showed a lady with a flowery hat perched over one eye, apparently in the act of lunging at a builder with a pole. The vicar stared at it in disbelief. As his cup filled up and overflowed onto the table, his eye moved unwillingly to the headline. VICAR'S WIFE IN BRAWL WITH BUILDERS. He gargled for a moment before finding his voice. 'Mildred,' he called. 'Could we have a word please?'

27

'I've got it!' Archie sat up in his chair.

'Well, I hope it's not contagious,' said Ruby.

'Those initials in Fred's notebook. You were able to put names to all of them except SP. Maybe that's because SP isn't a person at all but something else.'

'That's SE.'

'What is?'

'Something else.'

'I meant SP could be something other than a person.'

'Such as?'

'Such as Stolen Property.'

'Do you really think so?'

'Well, think about it,' said Archie.' We know that Bradley forced Gino into committing a burglary, but it left him with a problem. How does he get rid of the loot? A professional thief would know, but the chances are that Bradley hasn't a clue. All he could do would be to hide it somewhere until he finds a way of turning it into cash. If Fred suspected that this is what happened, it would explain the notes in his little book, i.e. "SP. Garage" simply means Bradley has the stolen property in his garage.'

'So you're saying this Cora necklace thing could be hidden there?'

'Exactly. It needs checking, don't you think? And what's more, Al Richards says Bradley disappears on Saturday nights. Maybe that's because he's searching for a buyer, possibly in one of the big cities.'

'Aren't you getting a bit carried away, Archibald?'

'Well, it all seems to fit.'

'Maybe. All I can say is that Fred didn't talk about his suspicions to me. He once told me it was best if I didn't know too much. He thought it was safer.'

'Good for him. Anyway, there's nothing to stop me following up the idea.'

'What do you mean? You're not going to go poking about in Bradley's garage, are you?'

'I don't know what I'll be doing yet, Aunt Ruby. I need to think.'

'Well, my advice would be to go to the police with your suspicions. Leave the investigating to the professionals.'

'That's okay if you have proof of some sort, but I don't. The police won't act on suspicions alone. They need proper evidence before they go searching people's property. I need to find out more.'

'That's exactly what's worrying me. You mustn't do anything silly.'

'Have you ever known me do anything silly?'

'Many times, Archibald. Would you like to hear about some of them?'

'Er, not just now, thanks. You don't want to dent my confidence do you? By the way, is Bradley out of hospital yet?'

'I believe he discharged himself when he woke up. Anyway, don't change the subject. Just be careful what you're doing.'

'Don't worry, I'll look before I leap. Decisions made in the heat of the moment often go wrong,' he said giving her a knowing look.

She nodded. 'Yes, all right Archie, I did get a bit carried away on that field. But poor Mildred! She got blamed for attacking Bradley although she was entirely innocent. It was an accident.'

'I believe you, but what can be done about it?'

'We can't undo what's done, but we can ask *The Echo* to print an apology.

'For what?'

'For making it look like a deliberate act, of course.'

'Well, good luck with that. *The Echo* won't be in any hurry to admit its mistake.'

'Archibald! Never underestimate the power of The Ladies Club. We can be very persuasive.'

'I don't doubt it. So, what do you propose to do then ... stage another demo?'

'I don't know. What we need before we do anything is some evidence. Something that will show it was all an accident.'

'Well at least we agree on that! Evidence is all important.

Anyway, I thought you said there were a lot of people there, so there'd be plenty of witnesses.'

'Yes, but how many can swear to what happened? It was all over in a flash.'

'That's true. So it boils down to your word against the newspaper's.'

They sat in gloomy silence as they thought this over.

'So,' said Archie eventually, 'remind me of what *The Echo* said. Did it actually accuse the vicar's wife of an attack on Bradley or was it more in the nature of innuendo?'

'No, it didn't accuse her in so many words. It simply published the photograph of Mildred appearing to strike him in the face alongside a headline that said "Vicar's Wife in Brawl with Builder".'

'Right then, they have a photograph but it should be one of many. Professional photographers usually take a series of shots so they don't miss anything. Then after printing, the editor can select what he wants.'

'So where does that get us?'

'Well, I don't know at the moment. The evidence may well be on their premises in a dark room or somewhere.'

They looked at each other. 'We need a plan, don't we Archie?'

'We certainly do, Aunt Ruby, but first, how about a tea break? It always helps the little grey cells to function.'

'Of course. And would an Eccles cake help?'

'Undoubtedly.'

'Right, then I'll put the kettle on.'

28

A pale yellow moon, appearing occasionally from behind the clouds, cast a rather ghostly light on the big Victorian pile that stood before them. Peering at it, Archie gave a low whistle. So this was the Bradley home. 'Quite a place,' he muttered. It was the first time he'd seen it, but he knew that it had once belonged to old Sam Bradley, Joe's father. Sam had bought it when it was neglected and falling into disrepair and he'd spent a lot of time and money, putting it in good order. Now that Sam had gone, Joe was the new owner.

'Well,' said Archie to the small figure standing beside him, 'What do you think?'

'I don' like it!' said Gino. 'I wanna go home.'

'Me too,' Archie agreed, 'but we're quite safe. He goes away at the weekends and won't be back until Sunday night.'

'Hey, how you know this, huh?'

'Don't worry, I have it on good authority. Anyway, let's just get on with it. It's no use getting cold feet at this late stage.'

'Hey, my feet ain't cold, I'm just nervous that's all ...' He looked fearfully around. 'Suppose he turns up and catches us? It's okay for you. You don' work for him.'

'I don't and I'm grateful for that small mercy,' said Archie, 'so let's not waste any more time. We'll take a look at the garage and you can tell me if it can be broken into.'

They walked to the end of the driveway where there was a big old building that looked as if it had been a stable block in a previous life. Archie produced a torch and they walked round it, inspecting as they went.

'So, what do you think, Gino?' Archie said. 'Is there a way in?'

'You're joking! It ain't got no windows and I no good at pickin' locks.'

'Right then, we'll have to move to plan B. We need the key.'

'Sure you do. Maybe he lend it you next time you see 'im, huh?'

'Or even quicker, we could find the spare one.'

'The spare one?'

Archie gestured towards the house. 'The one in there.'

Gino frowned as he thought about this. 'I no understand.'

'Well, doesn't everybody keep spare keys in the house?'

'Sure, maybe. But you need to get in da house first,' said Gino, putting his finger on a snag.

'Or someone could break in.'

As Gino took in the implications of this, his face fell. 'No way!' he said, a note of terror in his voice. 'If Bradley catch me in his house, he tear me apart!'

Archie put his arm round the little man's shoulders. 'Okay, calm down. Bradley is not going to catch you and I'm not asking you to go searching for a key. Just get the front door open and then you can go home. I'll do the rest. Anyway, let's take a look.'

They turned their attention to the house. After they'd inspected it all round, Archie shrugged his shoulders. 'Okay, maybe it'll be too difficult.'

At this last remark, Gino stiffened. 'Hey, what you mean, too difficult? I can see an open window. It easy.'

Archie craned his neck. 'Where? I can't see it.'

'On de roof.'

'What? Is that an open skylight? Can you manage that?'

'Sure I can manage dat. You want me to show you?'

'Yes, I'd like that very much.'

Archie watched as Gino made his way up the building using a succession of handholds and footholds on spouts, ledges, projections and anything else that assisted his progress. Soon his body was disappearing through the open skylight. 'Well done, little man,' Archie muttered admiringly. 'Pride conquers fear!'

When the front door eventually opened, Archie wasted no time in entering. 'Great, Gino,' he said, 'that was brilliant!'

'T'ank you. Anyt'ing else I can do?'

'No, I'm just pleased to see you've still got it. Okay, if you hang on until I've finished, I'll take you home. Otherwise, you'll have a long walk. It's about three miles back into town.'

'I t'ink maybe I go now. I no want to hang around here!'

Archie watched the little man as he crossed the field at the back of the house before disappearing into the darkness. He closed the door and set about the task of exploring the place.

Archie expected that a house owned by Joe Bradley would be comfortable, but as he explored he was amazed at the level of luxury. Expensive carpets, wallpapers, furniture and lighting were everywhere. The man who regularly provided third rate workmanship for his clients was unstinting when it came to himself. He took a look through a window. The house stood in extensive grounds surrounded by lawns, flowerbeds and trees, and was without any near neighbours, as far as he could see. After a minute or so of gawping at all this, Archie had to remind himself that he had work to do. 'So where to start searching?' he asked himself. He decided to make a start in the kitchen.

He was heading through the living area when a light appeared suddenly in the window. It moved across and got steadily brighter. Archie moved to the window and peered out from behind a curtain.

He saw a car approaching and he fully expected it to pass by on its way somewhere up the road. To his consternation, it turned in and came to a halt in the driveway. He could dimly make out a figure, sitting in driving seat. 'Just my luck,' he muttered, as he crouched behind the curtains. It looked as if Bradley was home early.

The car sat on the driveway for what seemed like an age, but eventually, the lights went off and the driver climbed out. He then stood there, examining the building as if looking for something. A moment later, someone else climbed out on the passenger side. They walked together towards the house, at the same time raising their arms to their heads. He realised they were putting on hats. Not just any old hats, but peaked caps.

He didn't know whether to be pleased or sorry. Instead of an encounter with a hostile builder, it looked as if he was faced with a visit from the Evesbury police. He wondered if he had inadvertently set off an alarm.

As the pair walked towards the house, he ducked down below the level of the windowsill. A light suddenly flashed on through the window and swept round the room.

'Just look at this!' said a voice. 'We're in the wrong job 'ere Bert.'

'Tell me about it,' said Bert. 'I was up 'ere a few weeks ago.'

'What, you mean this is a regular thing?'

'Seems like it. According to the Sarge, it's owned by Bradley the builder. He told the inspector he believes in crime prevention and that it's our job to keep an eye on the place when he's away.'

'Does he think we've nothin' better to do?'

'Seems like it but you know how it is with these fellers. They know what strings to pull. Anyway, don't knock it. Chance for a fag isn't it, Bert?'

'Good thinking. Have one of mine.'

'Ta.'

During this exchange, Archie could hardly believe his ears. He would have thought the police were the last people Bradley would want sniffing around his house. Surely he was having a laugh, wasn't he? Especially when his 'business' was probably getting rid of stolen goods. Then again, maybe he wanted to create an image of the respectable businessman. An honest man who didn't mind the law poking around his property.

Outside, a match flared and while the pair were lighting up, Archie tried to ease his cramped position by stretching out a leg. His foot hit against a small table parked under the window and for a split second he glimpsed a wobbling vase. As it fell sideways he made a grab, missed it and tensed himself for the crash. His heart meanwhile, did a back flip that Gino would have been proud of. Fortunately, the carpet had a deep pile and the vase fell with a soft thud, still apparently in one piece. Archie breathed a sigh of relief.

Outside, a voice suggested that it was time to get on with their tour of inspection, before they froze to death. 'Good idea,' Archie thought, 'and don't take too long.' As their voices faded away, Archie restored the vase to its position, and thanked his stars for soft carpets and for his foresight in parking the car down the lane, out of sight.

Getting stiffly to his feet, he found a chair in a quiet corner and settled down to wait for the moment when he was alone again. He heard noises as doors and windows were tried and tested for security. Eventually, the noises stopped, doors slammed, an engine started and the sound of the car faded into the distance. He rose from his chair, mopped his brow, and headed for the kitchen.

There, he found plenty of drawers and searched methodically through them by the light of his torch. In one, he came across an opened letter. The envelope was neatly typed and addressed to 'J. Bradley Esquire'. Archie regarded this with some surprise but he supposed business people had to be polite, even to the likes of Bradley.

He was returning the envelope to the drawer when the contents caught his eye. This was no business document, but a handwritten letter in blue ink. For a moment or two, he wrestled with his conscience. It looked like a personal letter and no business of his. On the other hand it could be of help in the battle. He had a moral duty, he told himself, to use any weapon he could. With that, his conscience saw his point, apologised for interfering and bowed out.

The letter, only a couple of pages long, was penned in thin spidery writing that was difficult to read. He couldn't make out the address properly but it seemed to be somewhere called Dunnley or Dummley. Whatever it was, he'd never heard of it. The rest of the letter was equally difficult to read but he did his best. It was the opening that caused Archie to blink.

"My Darling Joseph," it began.

'Darling?' He checked the envelope again to make sure it was addressed to Bradley. Satisfied that it did, he read on.

"What a lovely time we had last weekend darling. And thank you for that lovely bracelet, though I still don't understand why I can't wear it in public. After all, Honeybun, what use is it if you can't show it off?"

'Honeybun?' Archie could think of a variety of suitable names for the builder, but not that one. He could only conclude that either she'd had a brainstorm, or she was in love.

As for her complaint about being unable to wear the bracelet.

That was the trouble with stolen jewellery. It didn't do to put it on public display.

He read on with increasing disbelief. The Bradley she was talking about bore no resemblance to the Bradley he knew. The missive was peppered with endearments and some of it, he decided, would not be fit to repeat to his aunt. At the bottom, the scrawl was virtually unreadable. It said Your Ever Loving something, but he couldn't make out the signature.

By the time Archie had finished reading, he decided he'd had enough of this drivel. He put the letter back in the envelope and carried on with his search. It wasn't long before he found what he was looking for, a collection of keys in one corner of a drawer.

He selected a couple that looked right for the job and took them out to the garage. One of them turned the lock and he pulled open the door and stepped inside.

Using his torch, he could see a clear space in the centre, big enough for a car. Surrounding the space, there was a collection of items, none of it looking as if it came under the heading of Stolen Property. There was a paint-covered wooden ladder, a mix of scaffold equipment, some half-empty tins, two hard hats, cement in bags and a host of other miscellaneous junk. It was the sort of collection beloved of builders and decorators and not unlike the lot he'd found in the cellar of the Mayor's house.

He paused to think. He was not unduly surprised. While he'd been working on the theory that Bradley had been unable to shift the stuff, the recent reports of his weekend disappearances seemed to indicate that he'd finally found an outlet for it. Not only that, but it appeared he'd found a girlfriend into the bargain.

Shrugging off his disappointment, he decided it was time to go home.

He locked the garage door and took the keys back to the kitchen. He had another look at the love letter and wondered if he should take it with him. He decided against it. Whatever its value as evidence, he'd obtained it by committing a misdemeanour himself.

Without further ado, Archie made a quick check of his surroundings before heading for the front door.

As he drove home, he couldn't help feeling that somewhere along the line, he'd missed something. He decided it was time to give his brain a rest. Maybe a good night's sleep would stimulate that overworked organ.

29

'Well?' said Bradley.

'Well what, Joe?'

'You know what. Are we any further forward with this planning stuff?'

'It's not easy, Joe. These things can't be rushed.'

Bradley rubbed the bruise on his chin and gave Charlie Leggit a hard stare. 'You don't say. If you move any quicker, you'll be breaking into a crawl. So, what's the hold-up now?'

'It's the same problem, Joe. Objections have to be dealt with and it takes time. And that confrontation on The Meadow hasn't helped. After the newspaper report, most of the sympathy appears to be on the side of the women. The council are getting more letters criticising the scheme.'

'So the ones getting the sympathy are the ones who attacked me? What kind of logic is that?'

'I know, and I appreciate what you're saying. But public opinion is fickle. It was women against men and people in this country tend to support the underdog. We need to be careful. Anyway, all this talk is making me thirsty. Is there any tea on?'

'What do you think this is? Tiffin Time at the Ritz? This is a workshop and it doesn't run to entertaining guests. What I want to know is, how much longer can this go on? That field you sold me is a white elephant right now. If these delays drag on, I'll have to sell it back to the council.'

'I doubt if the council would be prepared to buy it, Joe. The money it raised has already been put aside for improvement work on council-owned houses. If they did buy it back, you'd probably only get a fraction of what you paid for it.'

Bradley gave him a dirty look. 'You what?' he said. 'In that case, *you'll* have to buy it, seeing that it was you who persuaded me to buy it in the first place.'

'You're joking, Joe. Where would I get that kind of money from?'

'I dunno, mate, that would be your problem. You got into this thing because you were looking to get a slice of the profits. Now you can share in the losses.'

'Steady on, Joe. No one is going to lose anything if we play our cards right. But I keep coming back to the main point. It'll take time.'

'And I keep telling you, I don't have time. Wages still have to be paid and the best I can hope for right now, is to sell some houses off-plan. I had some fool of a Frenchman looking at investing in some of the properties the other day, but he turned out to be like everyone else. All talk but no action.'

'Okay,' said the councillor, wondering how he could steer the conversation into calmer waters. 'I'm doing my very best in every way, Joe. I spent all last evening going carefully through those papers again. The ones taken from Oak Tree Cottage.'

'And?'

'I just thought you'd like to know.'

'No, I don't, unless you found something useful. Did you?'

'Er, I don't think so. As I mentioned before, the only interesting thing is what's missing rather than what's actually there.'

'So you said last time, and where exactly did that get us?'

'Yes, all right Joe. But how was I to know ...?'

'All right, all right, councillor, never mind the excuses. So, is there anything else?'

'No, not really. However, I have this feeling that I've missed something.'

'What thing?'

'Well, if I knew that Joe, I wouldn't be wondering, would I?'

'So, all you've got is some sort of feeling. A fat lot of good that is to me.'

'I know, I know and I'm sorry but just give me a bit more time to think. Perhaps a cuppa tea would help.'

'Would it? Well in that case, get yourself down to the tea room in Evesbury. Ask them for a pot of tea and a bucket of hot water. That should keep you going for a bit. In the meantime, maybe I can get on with something useful.'

30

In the offices of *The Evesbury Echo*, Philip Parker, the editor, was thinking about how to increase the sales of his rather boring newspaper. Sir Roscoe Hornby, the paper's owner had made it clear he wanted the paper livened up, and that one possible way would be to make it a touch more spicy. This had shaken the editor out of his normal complacency and sent him into a period of deep thought.

So, when he received the report of the confrontation on The Meadow, he'd spent a lot of time thinking about presentation. The result was a front page spread, complete with photograph, of a man being felled by a single blow to the head from a pole-wielding vicar's wife. There was no direct accusation, but the write-up and the picture made it look like a deliberate attack, The story caused the circulation of *The Echo*, to rise spectacularly.

Although pleased at this result, the editor realised it was a one-off and he wasn't going to get a story like that every week. Therefore, he reasoned, he must find a way of livening up the paper in a more permanent way. How this could be done was causing the editor a lot of short-tempered head scratching.

Finally, after much tea and biscuit-fuelled thought, he made up his mind. What he needed, he decided, was a regular gossip column of the kind seen in so many popular daily newspapers.

Having reached this conclusion, he wasted no time in getting into action. As no one on his present staff looked capable of taking on the role of gossip columnist, he decided there was no alternative but to advertise. So, the next edition of the paper carried an ad seeking, 'Someone with good literary skills, capable of writing regular reports on the more esoteric aspects of life in the area.'

The early responses were not encouraging. A couple of applicants were interviewed but neither appeared suitable. So, when his receptionist rang to say that a lady was in the lobby, wanting to see him, he hoped it might be third time lucky. 'What is she like?' he asked.

'Mrs Manning seems like a very feisty lady,' said the reception-ist.

'Send her up at once,' said the editor.

Ruby was ushered in and greetings exchanged. 'I'm very pleased to see you,' he told her.

'Are you?' said Ruby, a bit surprised. 'I won't say the same about you but I did want to talk to you.'

'Of course,' said the editor affably, 'It's the only way to conduct a job interview.'

'Job interview? What job interview?'

'You mean you are not here about the gossip column?'

'Gossip column? What gossip column?'

'Never mind,' said the editor hastily. 'It seems we have a misunderstanding. So what are you here about?'

'I'm here to make a complaint.'

The editor's manner became markedly less affable. 'You should have said so at reception. They would have dealt with it.'

'I doubt it. It's an editorial matter.'

'Even so ...! Anyway, what is the nature of this complaint?'

'There's been an injustice and I want it dealt with. Normally, me being me, I would be banging your desk and demanding action. However, my nephew has suggested I should try to keep calm and put my case in a reasonable manner, so that is what I'm doing.'

'I'm pleased to hear it,' said the editor, peering at her over the top of his half-moon glasses. 'But whether I can do anything depends on the nature of the problem. If, for instance, you feel you should have won our "Spot the Ball" competition but failed to do so, then I have to refer you to our independent arbitrator whose word is, I'm afraid, final. On other matters, I may or may not be able to help.'

'Who,' asked Ruby with some slight asperity, 'said anything about spot the ball, whatever that is? I didn't come here to talk about balls, spotted or otherwise. I came here to put something right. You are the editor, are you not, and therefore responsible for what gets published?'

'Well yes, as editor I do have a responsibility for what's published but sometimes, even I can be overruled. So what exactly, are we talking about here?'

'We are talking about that disgraceful piece in the last edition of *The Echo* accusing the vicar's wife of assault. She did not assault anybody. What happened was a complete accident.'

'I don't think many people would agree with you. The photographic evidence is indisputable.'

'Well I'm disputing it.'

'The camera doesn't lie.'

'In this case it does. Mildred Crouch would never hurt a fly. What happened was purely accidental.'

'Well, what do you want me to do? Tell our readers not to believe the evidence of their own eyes? That would make me look foolish.'

'Not half as foolish as you'll look when the truth comes out.'

'I'll take that chance. Now if you don't mind ...'

'Oh but I do mind,' said Ruby. 'I'd like you to check with the people who saw the whole thing and they'll tell you that it was an accident. Then you can print a full apology and we can forget the whole thing.'

'I'm sorry madam, but that isn't going to happen. Now, if you don't mind, I have a lot to get on with. However, please do have a complimentary cup of coffee in reception on your way out.'

'Right,' said Ruby, 'In that case, I have only one more thing to say to you.'

'What's that then?'

'THAT YOU HAVEN'T HEARD THE LAST OF THIS,' she bawled at the top of her voice, thumping the editor's desk to give emphasis.

31

It was beginning to get dark as Bradley's pick-up truck drove into the car park at Evesbury police station. Councillor Leggit was looking forward to stretching his legs after being obliged to share his seat with a bag of cement.

'Are you sure this is a good idea?' said Bradley, as they got out.

'The way I see it Joe, we've nothing to lose. You and your men were working on land that you own and then those women came along with the intention of causing trouble. They can't be allowed to get away with it.'

'I hope you're right Councillor. I've got better things to do than hang around police stations. They make me nervous.'

'Don't worry, let's just go in and see what they have to say.'

Inside, Sergeant Bowden glanced at his watch and saw that his shift still had an hour or so to go. So far, it had been a drag. He'd dealt with enough reports, arrests and complaints to fill three episodes of a police drama and in the process his mug of tea had gone cold.

Councillor Leggit approached the desk, having donned his most ingratiating expression. 'Good evening, Sergeant,' he said.

The sergeant, being a well-trained officer, resisted the urge to tell this smug-looking intruder to get lost, and instead confined himself to asking how he could help.

'We've come to report a crime.'

'Well then, you've come to the right place. What sort of crime?'

'An assault.' Here, Councillor Leggit felt he should show his familiarity with legal procedures and jargon. 'This,' he said, motioning Bradley to step forward, 'is Exhibit A.'

Bradley wasn't at all sure he liked being described as an exhibit, whether A, B or Z. He stepped reluctantly forward.

The sergeant regarded him dispassionately. 'At which particular part of Exhibit A are we supposed to be looking?' he enquired.

'Why the chin of course. Can't you see that massive bruise?'

'I see. Well this is a police station. Shouldn't you be at the hospital? They have a very good A and E department.'

'He's already been in hospital, having been knocked out by the blow. I'm showing you this as evidence of an assault while it's still fresh.'

'I see. And does the owner of the exhibit have a name?'

Bradley didn't like the tone of the proceedings. 'The name's Bradley,' he snarled, 'Joseph Bradley, taxpayer and a close acquaintance of your inspector.'

The sergeant nodded. 'Yes, I have heard him mention that name. Now, sir, can you give me some details of what exactly happened?'

'I was attacked.'

'Attacked by what?'

'A pole.'

'I see. You're sure about that?'

'Of course I'm sure, why shouldn't I be?'

'Well, it's not always easy to tell. It could have been a German or a Ukrainian or whatever. They all look pretty much alike.'

'Oh, very funny,' Bradley said. 'Well this one was long and thin and made of wood. And while you're in a humorous mood, is this a real police nick or are you in fancy dress?'

Councillor Leggit was quick to intervene. 'Please, let us not get at cross purposes on this,' he said. 'Mr Bradley is not here to waste your time. He just feels you should take some action on his behalf.'

'That is what we do in here. Our days are full of action such as checking on houses when the owners are away.'

Bradley nodded. 'I should hope so. I believe in crime prevention.'

'Rest assured,' said the sergeant, 'we are very keen on crime prevention too, though it does cost a fair bit. Fortunately for our budget, many owners of big properties round here have made their own security arrangements.'

Bradley shot the sergeant one of his looks. 'Have they? Well I pay too. It's called taxation.'

'I think,' said Councillor Leggit, 'we should get back to the matter in hand.'

'Right,' said the sergeant. 'Can you give me a description of the alleged assailant.'

'There's nothing alleged about her. She's the leader of a gang of women known, I'm told, as The Ladies Club.'

'And does this gang leader have a name?'

'It's Mrs Crouch, the vicar's wife,' said Leggit helpfully.

'Mildred Crouch?' queried the sergeant. 'The kindest, most compassionate woman in these parts?' He raised a quizzical eyebrow.

'We're just giving you the facts,' said Bradley, 'You're supposed to gather the evidence, not argue about it.'

'So, you wish to register a complaint alleging that Mrs Crouch attacked you. Is there anything else?'

'Yes. There was one other woman who was particularly aggressive. In fact I think she was the main troublemaker. She lives in Oak Tree Cottage in Gently.'

'You mean Ruby Manning?' said the sergeant in astonishment. 'The late Sergeant Manning's wife?'

It was Bradley's turn to be surprised. 'She was married to a policeman?'

'Not just any policeman. The best we've had round here. He taught me all I know.'

'Is that so?' said Bradley. 'I don't suppose that took very lon ...'

'Mr Bradley is aware of the situation,' said the councillor hastily. 'But as a policeman's wife, we feel Mrs Manning ought to have known better. So what are you going to do about it?'

'I'll have a word with the inspector in the morning. In the meantime, if that's all, I'd like to get some work done.'

As the pair made their way out, the sergeant turned to PC Draper. 'Take a tip from me, laddie, and keep your eye on those two,' he said. 'But right now, get that kettle on before I die of thirst.'

32

The following day, Ruby was clearing away the breakfast things while Archie attended to the fire. 'I've had a tip off,' she announced. It was an expression she'd picked up from the crime story she was currently reading.

'A tip off? Can you elaborate?'

'Sergeant Bowden got a message to me, to tell me that Joe

Bradley intends to get me charged with assault.'

Archie gazed at her in astonishment. 'You, charged with assault? I don't believe it! And who is this Sergeant Bowden?'

'A friend. He trained under Fred.'

'I see, but how can you be accused of assault? It was actually the vicar's wife who struck the blow, wasn't it? The proof was all over the newspaper.'

'True, but it seems that I could be charged as an accessory. Though how you can be an accessory to an accidental trip is a mystery to me.'

'But the trouble is, it doesn't look accidental in the picture. It shows Bradley being struck on the chin by a woman wielding a pole. I take it you are familiar with the old saying, "the camera doesn't lie"?'

'You're as bad as the editor,' said Ruby. 'That's what he said, so I told him to check his photos again and to talk to the people who were there.'

'And has he done?'

'I don't know, but I doubt it. Even if he found out it was an accident, he'd hardly go shouting it around, would he? It would only show him in a bad light.'

'Right,' said Archie. 'This is a case for Inspector Graham, I think. I'll do a bit of lobbying around the newspaper staff. They might be a bit more forthcoming than the editor. I mean, it stands to reason that they'll have more than one photograph. You never know what other evidence they could have.'

Ruby looked doubtful. 'I appreciate that, Archie, but I don't see how you'll persuade anyone on the paper to risk their job by producing proof of that sort.'

'Okay, but it's worth a try.'

'Do you even know anyone on the staff?'

'Not a soul.'

'Oh great, then you're off to a flying start then, aren't you?'

'But I do know someone who seems to know everyone in these parts. I'll ask.'

'Right, so who is this someone then?'

'Maisie, of course.'

Ruby looked at the clock 'I thought Maisie might come into it somewhere. She'll be in the pub this lunchtime, won't she?'

'That's just what I was thinking.'

'Well?' said Ruby as Archie returned that afternoon.

'Very well thanks. How's yourself?'

'Archie, just tell me what happened.'

'Sorry, Aunt. Well, Maisie put me in touch with a girl who works on the paper and I've had a chat with her. Her name is Sarah. Maisie and I met her over a sandwich at the Rainbow Café in Evesbury.'

'And?'

'And she seemed very suspicious. She talked a lot about confidentiality and all that. In the end, I said it would be good to talk more about the ethics of the situation, so I invited her out for a meal. After a good deal of hesitation, she agreed.'

'An evening out? Can you afford it?'

'I think so. I know where there's a very good chippy in Evesbury and we can join in the singalong in The Highwayman afterwards.'

'Wow!' said Ruby. 'You certainly know how to spoil a girl.'

33

From his position in the public gallery, the Reverend Bernard Crouch looked nervously down at the courtroom. He'd never known a situation like this before and he was struggling to take it all in. Who would have thought that when his wife set out on a peaceful protest march, she would end up in a courtroom? Of course, he had every faith that she'd done nothing wrong, but there was nothing he could do about it except pray. He turned to a mournful-looking chap sitting nearby.

'What do you think the chances are?' he asked, hopefully.

Corky looked puzzled, 'Chances of what?'

'The chances of the defendant getting off.'

'Dunno mate,' said Corky. 'I couldn't tell you much about it, except what I've read in the paper. I'm only here to support Archie.'

'Archie?'

'Archie Graham, the defendin' counsel. A friend of mine.'

'Really. Which one is he?'

'Right there,' said Corky, pointing a finger, 'the one in a dark suit, sittin' at the desk.'

'I see. He's good at this is he? Defending the innocent?'

'Dunno,' said Corky. 'He says he's never done anything like this before.'

The vicar paled. 'What do you mean, he's never done this before? You mean he's not a lawyer?'

'Oh he's a lawyer all right, but accordin' to what he told me, he's only ever worked for the British Embassy abroad. He says his speciality is international law, not criminal cases.'

'Then what on earth is he doing here?'

'His aunt persuaded him. She's in the dock along with some vicar's wife.'

The Vicar looked even more alarmed. 'Yes, I'm that vicar and she's my wife!' As he slumped in his seat, he murmured, 'Mildred, what have they done to you?'

'I think the case is more about what she did to that builder,' said Corky, helpfully. 'Knocked 'im out cold, according to what I 'eard.'

'It was an accident.'

'No offence, Vicar,' said Corky, 'but they all say that, don't they?'

At that moment, there was a sudden flurry of activity in the room. 'All rise!' the Usher called and everyone rose obediently as the three magistrates filed in. They took their seats on the bench and the rest of the court followed suit.

The chief magistrate, Hubert Irwin JP, leant down for a word with The Clerk of the Court, Josh Sayers. 'What do we have today, Mr Sayers?'

'A case of assault and initiating a riot, sir. Two defendants, Mrs Ruby Manning and Mrs Mildred Crouch.'

'Really? We've had too many of these violent incidents lately. It's time we made an example of such offenders and I'm sure my colleagues will feel the same.' He glared at the two other magistrates who nodded in agreement, not wishing to incur the wrath of the famously peppery Hubert.

'Only if they're guilty, of course,' said the fair-minded Josh.

'Oh, I think there's a good chance they're guilty. I admit they don't look the type, but the more innocent they look, the worse they are in my experience. Anyway, let's get on with it.'

The clerk addressed the defendants. 'You are Mrs Mildred Crouch of The Vicarage, Woodlands Road, Evesbury?'

'I am.'

'And you are Mrs Ruby Manning of Oak Tree Cottage, Meadow Lane, Gently.'

'You know I am, Josh,' said Ruby. How's your mother these days?'

There was an outbreak of sniggering in the room followed by some irate banging of His Honour's gavel. 'Silence in court! Just answer the question Mrs Manning.'

'If you say so,' said Ruby.

'Usher, if you please.'

The Usher came forward and spoke to Ruby. 'Take the book in your right hand and repeat after me, "I swear to tell the truth, the whole truth and nothing but the truth".'

'I always do,' said Ruby. 'Within reason, of course,' she added, primly.

'Just repeat the words please.'

'I swear to tell the truth, the whole truth and nothing but the truth.'

In the gallery, Corky shook his head. 'Oh, dear, oh dear!' he said.

'What?' asked the vicar anxiously 'Well, WHAT?'

'It's old Irwin,' said Corky. 'He's a tough nut if ever there was one. Gave me a hefty fine for not 'avin' a TV licence and threatened me with gaol if I ever did it again. An' all because I forgot about it. I was totally innocent.'

'Don't they all say that?' enquired the vicar.

The Clerk of the Court read out the charge which was to the effect that the pair in the dock had attacked a group of builders in the village of Gently, causing a riot and actual bodily harm to one of their number, a Mr Joseph Bradley.

'How do you plead, Guilty or Not Guilty?' enquired the Clerk.

'Not Guilty!' they chorused.

In the public seats, Corky shook his head again. 'Big mistake,' he said. 'They go a lot easier on you if you admit it straight away.'

'Why doesn't their lawyer say something?' the vicar asked. 'And who is that sitting by him. They seem to have a lot to say to each other.'

'That's the Major,' said Corky. 'Ex-army bloke.'

The vicar brightened. 'Really? You mean an army lawyer, or someone who worked for the army legal department?'

'Nah. The Major was infantry.'

'Good heavens, so why is he assisting the defence?'

'No reason. He volunteered because he's a mate. We're all pals together, me, Archie and the Major meet in the pub.'

The vicar put his head in his hands. 'Oh dear, what a shambles. The blind leading the blind.'

'Too right Vicar,' said Corky gloomily.

The prosecuting council, Mr Leonard Critchley, got to his feet. 'On what grounds are you denying the charge?'

'The grounds that we didn't do it,' boomed Mrs Crouch. 'We would never do such a thing.'

'At this point, Your Honour,' said Critchley, 'I would like to show the court Exhibit A, the kind of weapon used in the attack.'

'Very well. Proceed.'

The usher brought in a pole with its attached board.

'Is this the sort of weapon used?'

'Yes, Your Honour, it is identical.'

'Objection!' Archie was on his feet. 'This is not the original. None of the ladies carried that banner. The fact that it says STUFF THE POLL TAX is a clue. Shows it has been borrowed from another occasion entirely.'

There was a moment's silence. 'Objection sustained,' Mr Hubert Irwin said eventually and with some reluctance. 'Usher, remove the exhibit please.'

Leonard Critchley was not to be deterred. 'If it pleases the court, I would now like to show Exhibit B, a photograph of the actual assault. This clearly shows the defendants charging towards Mr Bradley with one of them actually striking him in the face with the sort of weapon previously described.'

'This,' Ruby interrupted, 'was a peaceful protest, not the Charge of the Light Brigade. The whole thing was an accident and what you are calling weapons, were simply boards with messages on them.' She turned towards the Clerk. 'You know the sort of thing, Josh. You see them on protest marches all the time.'

His Honour banged the gavel again. He gave Ruby a deeply disapproving look. 'Please confine yourself to answering the questions Mrs Manning. Pray continue, Mr Critchley.'

'Thank you, Your Honour.' The prosecutor paused while the photograph was passed around for examination. Turning to the dock, the prosecutor said, 'You, Mrs Crouch, were the one who struck Mr Bradley the near fatal blow?'

'Objection!' Archie spoke again. 'There is no evidence to suggest that the blow was anywhere near fatal.'

'More's the pity,' muttered Ruby.

'Objection sustained,' His Honour said.

On the defence's table, Archie turned to his colleague. 'Any word from Sarah at *The Echo*?' he asked in a low voice.

'Afraid not, old boy,' the Major whispered back.

'She promised she'd consider sending me more photographs.'

At that moment, an envelope was passed to Archie. 'About

time,' he murmured, ripping it open. As he studied it, his face fell.

'Something the matter?' enquired the Major.

'I'm afraid Sarah's chickened out,' said Archie. 'Says the photos belong to the paper and she'd be sacked if they found out she'd shown them outside the office.'

'Oh I say! Bad luck old boy. Anything I can do?'

'Not really. And, I'm just wasting your time keeping you here, Major. Your time would be far better spent on continuing your search for new digs.'

The Major hesitated. 'Well, if you're sure.'

'I'm sure and thanks for your help.'

'Absolute pleasure,' said the Major, before sliding out of his seat and making quietly off.

Left alone, Archie admitted to himself that the prospects were not good. Without photographic evidence, his chances looked decidedly slim. But, he would do his best.

Witnesses came and went. For Bradley, a couple of his men testified to seeing the incident as a deliberate attack. For the defendants, a couple of ladies spoke of the excellent characters of those in the dock and described the incident as a pure accident. As for the 'riot', both sides agreed that the incident fell more into the category of handbags at dawn, rather than anything more serious. Throughout this period, a puzzled Bradley kept shooting glances at Archie and wondering where he'd seen him before.

Finally, the magistrate announced that he and his colleagues would withdraw to confer. As things stood, he said, the only evidence of a substantive nature was the photograph showing two females rushing towards Mr Joseph Bradley with one of them in the act of striking him with a wooden pole. However, he said, he intended that he and his colleagues would consider all the arguments and come back with a decision. With that, the magistrates withdrew, leaving an atmosphere of gloom to hover over the defence team's bench.

It was at this point that the Major made an unexpected return.

34

'I've made you a special cake,' said Ruby.

'What?' Archie was jerked out of his sleep in front of the roaring fire.

'A cake! The sort you like. Lots of fruit in it.'

'It's not my birthday. Not for another couple of months anyway.'

'I know that. This is to celebrate getting me and Mildred off the hook.'

Archie pushed his chair back a bit. 'That heat keeps sending me off. I'd begun to dream that Bradley was in the stocks and that you were throwing rotten fruit at him.'

'Did I hit him?'

'I'll never know. You woke me up at the critical moment.'

'I bet I did. I wouldn't miss an opportunity like that. Anyway, you did well for us Archie. Didn't I tell you, you could do it?'

'Yes, but more by good luck than anything else. You have the Major to thank really.'

'He brought in those photographs, didn't he?'

'Yes, but it wasn't that simple. Sarah, at *The Echo* office, had already decided not to let me have them. The Major went to see her and managed to get her to change her mind.'

'How did he do that?'

'That's what I'm waiting to find out.'

'He probably offered her a better night out than a meal at the chip shop.'

'Don't remind me. But you always told me to live within my means, Aunt Ruby. Next month will be different. I'll be starting my new job.'

She sighed. 'I know, and I'm going to miss you.'

'Don't worry. I'll only be a few miles away, so I can still come and see you.'

'Make sure you do. Anyway, the next time you see him, give my thanks to the Major.'

'I certainly will, if he's not too busy.'

'Busy with what?'

'Well, it seems that he'll be seeing Sarah from *The Echo* again.'

'Really? It sounds as if a romance is blossoming.'

'It could be. I know he'd like to marry, and get away from his present accommodation. It's sub-standard and comes with a free personal account of his landlady's latest ailments.'

'Hmm,' Ruby looked doubtful. 'I'm not sure that sounds like the basis for a good marriage. Anyway, let's hope it works out for him. Just tell him I'm grateful he got hold of those photos. They proved our case.'

'They certainly did. In particular, the one that showed Mrs Crouch tripping over one of Bradley's string lines.'

'It shouldn't have come to a trial. Anyone with half an eye should have seen she isn't capable of acts of violence, especially biffing anyone in the face with a pole. Even someone as foul as Joe Bradley.'

'I agree, but the law works on facts and evidence. Even with the photographic evidence, I think old Irwin was reluctant to find you Not Guilty. He'd made up his mind that your case would boost his reputation as a hard nut, and he was forced to deliver his Not Guilty verdict through gritted teeth. Anyway, all's well that ends well.'

'Except it's not the end,' said Ruby. 'Joe Bradley won't take this lying down. He'll be planning his next rotten move.'

'Maybe,' said Archie. 'But I can't think what else he can do.'

35

In the offices of *The Evesbury Echo*, the editor sat gloomily pondering the situation. A visit from Ruby Manning that morning had left him in no doubt that there was trouble ahead. What the court's 'Not Guilty' verdict meant, she said, was that he must print a full and grovelling apology in his rotten paper or face the consequences. She was, she declared, ready and willing to sue. With that, she swept off, leaving the editor to wonder how he could get out of this with his job and his dignity still intact. The short answer at this moment appeared to be that he couldn't.

He was deep in thought when the phone rang. He gave it a jaundiced look, barely resisting the impulse to rip it out and hurl it across the room. Instead, he decided to ignore it. When it failed to stop ringing, he picked it up and snarled 'Not now!' He was about to slam it down when he caught the word 'Hornby' issuing from the instrument.

'What?'

'Sir Roscoe has just pulled up in the yard.'

The editor's heart sank into his polished shoes. The last time the paper's owner, Sir Roscoe Hornby, had paid him a visit it was to give him a dressing down. On that occasion, the editor was told to liven things up or he would be handed his cards without further ceremony. Now, all that had backfired and the owner was bound to put all the blame on him. While all this was going through his mind, he heard footsteps on the stairs. In that instant, he made his mind up. It was time to assert himself and tell the tycoon exactly what he thought of him.

As soon as the door started to open, he waded in. 'Ah, Hornby!' he began, 'I've been wanting a word with ...'

He was cut short when Sir Roscoe's face appeared. It was wreathed in smiles.

'Philip my boy,' said the tycoon, extending a hand. 'How are you?'

The editor was struck dumb for a moment, 'Er, I'm very well Sir Roscoe,' he said as they shook hands, 'How are you?'

'Never better, thank you, never better. What was it you were saying as I came in?'

'Oh nothing, nothing Sir Roscoe. I was just expressing surprise at seeing you.'

'Of course, of course. But you know me. I like to keep in touch and all that, so I thought I'd drop in, especially as it's such a beautiful day.'

'Is it? I thought it was raining rather heavily.'

'Well yes, there is that, of course, but that's what keeps everything so fresh and green, does it not? Anyway, enough of that. How are things?'

'Er, well, there is a problem. The ...'

'Of course there's a problem. There always is in this business. But I leave it to your good self to sort it out. That's what I pay you for, is it not? Anyway, how are the wife and kids, hmm?'

'I don't have a wife or kids.'

'Don't you? Oh no, of course you don't. I'm mixing you up with that other idiot who runs my garden magazine. I had intended putting him on the spot today, but as it happens, I'm not in that sort of mood.'

'I had noticed. May I ask if there's a reason for so much good humour?'

'Ask, of course you may ask. Doesn't mean I'm going to tell you does it, ha! ha! The fact is, I've just had a remarkable piece of good fortune. I don't like boasting about these things of course, but when it involves a sum like er, a quarter of a million quid, well, that's really something isn't it?'

'Quarter of a mill ... how did that come about?'

The tycoon tapped the side of his nose with a pudgy finger. 'Acumen, my boy, business acumen. Some have it, some don't.'

'Tell me more.'

'Well not a lot to tell, really. I bought these chemical shares a year ago and now I've sold them and made a killing in the process.'

'That is great news! I hope it makes you happy.'

'Of course it makes me happy. Wouldn't you be happy with a windfall like that?'

'Absolutely. So can I take it you know all about that other little matter?'

'What other little matter?'

'Well, all that business with the builder, the vicar's wife and a wooden pole.'

'The builder, the vic ... have you been reading too many comic books lately?'

'Certainly not. Perhaps I'd better explain.'

'Perhaps you had.'

'Well, after you told me to make the paper more interesting, I published a photograph that showed a local builder being attacked by a group of women and, to cut a long story short, it's caused an almighty row. It has been suggested that we print an apology ... or else.'

'Or else what?'

'Or else we could, er, be sued. In fact we might be sued anyway.'

There was a silence during which the editor swallowed uneasily. 'Of course,' he said, eventually, 'compared with your recent windfall, the sum involved would be ...'

'And I suppose you sanctioned this photo?'

'Well, yes. I thought it was the kind of thing you would want.'

'Did you? Well perhaps you should have thought not only about the things I wanted, but about the things I *didn't* want, like being sued for instance.'

'It needn't actually come to that.'

'What do you mean, it needn't come to that?'

'Well, I'm told there'll be no need for a court case providing we print an apology and make a donation to the local hospital.'

There was another silence during which the tycoon lit a cigar. 'A donation, eh?' he said eventually, blowing out a cloud of smoke. 'Maybe that could be good publicity.'

'I agree,' said the editor eagerly, 'we could photograph you handing over the cheque.'

The tycoon considered this. 'Yes,' he said eventually. 'Of course, and I could also give a short speech, pointing out that even honest reporting sometimes goes wrong through no fault of its own.'

'Sounds good to me,' said the editor hopefully, eyeing the tycoon through the fog.

'Right,' said Sir Roscoe, 'but the question is ... how *big* a donation?'

The editor pondered. 'Well, it needs to be big enough to impress. About three?'

'I take it you mean three hundred, not just three, ha! ha! Yes that sounds about right,"

'Er, well, I was thinking more along the lines of three thousand.'

'Three thou ...' Sir Roscoe nearly choked on his cigar. 'Do you think,' he spluttered, 'that I'm made of money?'

'No, but it is, after all, only a small percentage of that windf ...'

'Never mind about any windfall, Parker. That's a private matter and no business of yours. Just think yourself lucky you've still got a job.'

'Of course, Sir Roscoe. Sorry I mentioned it.'

'I should think so.' The tycoon glared out at the now torrential rain. 'What a stinking awful day!' he said as he rose and moved to take his leave. 'Have you got an umbrella?'

'I'm afraid not.'

'Typical! Now I'll get soaked just walking back to the car.'

'Oh, I do hope so,' muttered the editor as the door slammed.

36

'I see you got your apology then,' said Archie, looking up from his copy of *The Echo*.

'And not before time,' said his aunt, tartly.

'Was it grovelling enough for you?'

Ruby sniffed. 'Not by a long chalk. The way they've presented it, you'd think they were the injured party. And that photograph of the owner, Sir Roscoe Whatnot, handing over a cheque to the hospital makes him look like some sort of hero instead of the grasping bonehead we all know him to be.'

Archie nodded his approval. 'A good description. So does this mean you'll be crossing swords with the editor again?'

'I wouldn't waste my time,' said Ruby. 'We've had an apology of sorts and the local hospital has benefitted, so let's leave it at that.'

'Right. At least we can now concentrate on this housing thing again. What we need is proof of wrongdoing.'

'We certainly do, and if Fred was still here, he'd get it one way or another.'

'You're right Aunt. There's a clue in those notes he left, but I haven't yet figured it out.'

'Well keep trying, Archibald ... although on second thoughts, maybe you should just forget it. You'll have enough to think about, getting ready for your new position.'

'Don't worry. They wouldn't have given me the job if they thought I couldn't handle it.'

'I'm delighted to hear it.'

'Why, thank you Aunt. Meanwhile, I'll keep my investigation going.'

'If you say so. What do you have in mind?'

'There's a few things I'd like to go over with you. For instance, is your insurance up to date?'

'Why? Are you thinking of bumping me off?'

'I'm not talking about life insurance but insurance on the cottage.'

'House insurance?'

'That's the one.'

'Well, I've always used Surefire.'

'Sounds like a reliable company.'

'They're good, except for one small thing.'

'What's that then?'

'Councillor Leggit works for them. Mind you, I've never had any dealings with him. I always go direct to their office in Evesbury.'

'I'm pleased to hear it. So is the policy up to date?'

She looked suddenly uncomfortable. 'Er, it should be.'

'I know it should be,' said Archie, 'but is it?'

'I'll check.'

'Are you really telling me that it isn't?'

'I never said that. Anyway, does it matter?'

'Well of course it matters.'

'All right, all right,' she said. 'But those premiums have been taking a big chunk out of my budget.'

'So you've stopped paying them. Since when?'

'Er, a few weeks ago.'

'Right,' said Archie, it's Friday night and they'll be closed, but I'll be down there first thing in the morning.'

'They're closed on a Saturday.'

'Okay. Monday morning then. It'll help if I have the last insurance document with me.'

'I'm afraid there isn't one.'

'Oh, why not?'

'It's one of things that went missing when the house was burgled.'

On Saturday morning, Charlie Leggit was in Joe Bradley's office to hear Bradley vent his frustration at the way things had turned out. He was in a rage about the way the court case had gone and, not for the first time, the councillor was getting the full force of the blast. He decided to try and divert attention.

'Okay Joe,' he said soothingly, 'but you know the old saying. 'Don't get mad, get even.'

'And just how do you propose doing that, Councillor?' snarled the builder.

'I'm going through those papers of hers again. I'm sure there must something we can use.'

'You've been through them a hundred times. You won't find anything different.'

'Maybe, maybe not. There's no harm in trying.'

'Well, get on with it then. I've got better things to do.' The builder turned his attention to the pile of papers on his desk.

For several minutes there was silence, but for the rustling of paper. The councillor suddenly paused. 'Do you know Joe, I think I *have* been missing something.'

'What?'

'I've kept seeing the insurance papers on the cottage but not noticing the date properly. These are out of date by a few weeks.'

Bradley suddenly looked interested. 'Are you saying she has no up-to-date insurance on the house?'

'Well, not exactly. She may have up-to-date papers somewhere else.'

'Why should she? All the other papers are here, aren't they?'

'Not necessarily. Remember, her marriage certificate must be in a different place.'

'All right Councillor, forget what should or shouldn't be there. Can you just find out whether the cottage is insured or not?'

'I can tomorrow. She uses Surefire, the company I work for. I don't handle her actual account, but I can soon check at the office.'

'Good. I look forward to hearing from you.'

37

It was Sunday evening and Archie was gently dozing in front of the fire. He knew there was a word to describe his condition and his mind was searching for it. 'Ah!' he said suddenly. 'Replete ... that's the one.'

'What are you talking about Archibald?' Ruby asked, from the comfort of her rocking chair.

'Nothing important Aunt. I was searching for the right word to describe my feeling after another of your splendid meals. I think "replete" fills the bill.'

'Does it? Sounds a bit posh to me. Fred always called my cooking "gradely", a word he got from his Yorkshire father.'

'And quite right too. There's no doubt it's gradley.'

'Thank you, but you might not feel that way when you've put on a few pounds.'

'Let's not think about that now. Suppose we round off the evening by raising a glass to Uncle Fred. I could open those two bottles of ale I found in his shed?'

'Let's do that.'

Archie heaved himself out of his chair. 'Right then, after that I won't stay up too late. I must be up early to fix that insurance.'

'There's no need to rush, Archie. Nothing's going to happen.'

'I'm sure you're right.' He moved towards the kitchen. 'But let's not take any chances eh?'

In the kitchen he found a bottle opener and was about to start on the first bottle when he became aware of a light flickering in the window. Looking out, he saw a large bonfire in the garden.

'Hey, Aunt Ruby!' he called. 'I didn't know you were burning rubbish outside.'

There was a moment of silence. 'Burning rubbish? What are you talking about?'

'You mean you don't know we have a fire going in the garden?'

'Of course not.' She came bustling in and stood by him at the window. 'Oh, no!' she said suddenly, and bolted out of the door.

'What is it?' said Archie, a couple of steps behind.

'Fred's shed! It's on fire!'

38

They stared at the blazing building in horror. 'Water!' said Archie, 'we need water.'

Ruby came out of her daze. 'The well,' she said. 'We must fill some buckets.'

They rushed to the well and got busy, pumping up the water by hand. The well was conveniently near the house, but at some distance from the shed. It was clear that when Fred picked a spot for the shed, he'd opted for isolation over convenience. He probably thought that made it more like a retreat.

While this remoteness had suited Fred's purpose, it was not so good for carrying buckets of water in a hurry. Added to that was the fact that they'd recently finished a rather filling meal and they were soon puffing and wheezing their way along, slopping water all the way. They threw the contents of their buckets at the flames which spluttered and snarled for a short while before leaping up again.

'What we really need is running water,' gasped Archie as they passed each other.

'Well, I've got water and I'm running,' said Ruby as she puffed in the opposite direction.

It soon became obvious that they were fighting a losing battle. In a while they both stopped and stared as the few remaining bits of timber collapsed inwards to be consumed. Finally, all that remained were the metal bits of items such as garden tools and sadly, the framework of Fred's old chair. 'To think,' said Ruby, 'that I took the trouble to put that old rake you trod on away in there.'

'Ah!' said Archie, 'so it's not been all bad then.'

'This must be another of Joe Bradley's tricks.'

'Well, I'm sure it wasn't spontaneous combustion.'

It was suddenly all a bit much for Ruby. She stared at the smoking ruin for a while before turning away and taking a step towards the house. Then she let out a cry of anguish.

'Don't take it so hard,' said Archie. 'I know you had fond memories of it, but it was only a shed after all.'

'The house, Archie, the house!'

He turned to look. They had rushed out of the kitchen door, leaving the door open and through the door he saw flames. The kitchen was on fire!

Archie dashed to the kitchen door and saw flames licking up the side of the big dresser that stood against one wall. 'We've been conned!' he yelled. 'The shed was just a diversion. More water, quick!'

They were soon back to running between fire and well, but this time over a shorter distance. Unfortunately, the delay between one bucketful and the next was long enough allow the fire to still creep upwards towards to the roof. The delays were getting longer as the pair became more exhausted and nearer to the point of collapse.

Archie decided suddenly to try another tactic. Throwing his bucket on one side, he picked up the jacket he'd abandoned earlier and started to beat at the flames. This method brought some success as he began beating out the fire, his arm going like a flail. Then things changed when his jacket suddenly caught fire and he took on the appearance of a large Catherine wheel at a bonfire celebration. Eventually, he was forced to throw the flaming jacket into the garden before leaning against the wall with sweat pouring out of him as he gasped in air as fast as his lungs could take it.

He could see just how hopeless the situation had become. They were miles from help, there was no telephone, the only water came in a bucket and the fire was raging its way up to the thatched roof. Of Ruby there was no sign and he assumed that, having given her all, she'd given up the fight, and who could blame her? The flames would soon be into the roof and that spelt doom. The uninsured cottage was about to be burnt to the ground and there was nothing he could do about it.

In among the nearby trees, a shadowy figure stood watching the scene. He waited until the fire had taken a hold and the occupants were too exhausted to continue their efforts to put it out. With a grunt of satisfaction, Dooley turned away and headed for the village.

39

When Bradley's phone rang, he was quick to grab it off the hook. A short conversation followed and when he replaced the receiver, he looked like the cat who'd got the cream. He treated Charlie Leggit to one of his pleased looks. It wasn't a look that his face was accustomed to wearing, but it did its best. 'Well that's that little problem sorted, councillor,' he said, 'and not before time.'

'So what's happened now, Joe?' the councillor wanted to know. He wasn't too pleased at being dragged out to see Bradley so late of an evening, but he was curious to know why. Also, the fact that they were in Bradley's rather opulent residence rather than his usual grotty workshop went some way to appeasing him.

'What's happened, Councillor, is that the obstacle to progress has been removed. Widow Twankey has lost her cottage.'

The councillor gaped. 'What do you mean, lost her cottage?'

'Exactly that. The cottage has gone, kaput, burnt out. Not only that, but if the information you gave me is correct then she won't get a pennyworth of insurance for it. Would you like a whisky?'

The councillor wasn't sure which was the more amazing, the news about the cottage or the offer of a drink from the tightwad.

'Er, yes. Thank you Joe. So you arranged all this did you?'

Bradley busied himself with pouring the drinks. 'Did I say that? All I can say is that the phone call was from someone who has just witnessed the fire. When last seen, it was well alight and about to take that thatched roof with it.' He grinned. 'It seems they were trying to put it out with the occasional bucket of water.'

'I see.' Charlie Leggit wasn't at all sure it was good news. He was the arch manipulator and bender of rules, but this made him nervous. 'Are you sure about this, Joe?' he asked.

'Sure I'm sure. Are you getting the wind up, Councillor?'

'Er, no but arson is a serious matter. The police and the insurance companies will investigate a suspicious fire very thoroughly.'

'Not in this case. The place was uninsured. You told me that yourself.'

'That still leaves the police.'

'Yeah, yeah but fires in thatched roof cottages are not uncommon in these parts. A spark from the chimney is enough to start the whole thing off. I could say something to that effect to my friend the inspector at Evesbury nick.'

The councillor looked alarmed. 'Be very careful Joe. If I were you I wouldn't mention anything about it. Especially to the police. The less said the better. Er, who did the actual deed? Are you sure they can be relied on to keep quiet?'

The builder looked at him with a cynical smile. 'My, my, we are getting windy aren't we, Councillor? Are you sure you're still up for this? As for who did it, that's my business. Let's just say he's not in any position to go blabbing to anyone. Now, isn't it time you were getting home? You'll have a busy day tomorrow getting that planning sorted.'

Councillor Leggit got to his feet. He didn't like any of this but at the end of the day he was committed. At least it brought nearer the time when all this paid off and he got his cut. He was looking forward to it. If he concentrated on that, he thought, he might be able to sleep tonight.

40

'Here, grab hold of this!'

Archie came out of his daze to see Ruby standing near. 'What?'

'Just take this.'

'What is it?'

'It's a hosepipe, what does it look like?'

He took hold of it. 'Great! It'll come in handy when you get the mains water connected.'

'Stop talking and aim at the fire.'

'Anything to oblige.' He stood with it pointing at the blaze while she bustled off. He was amazed to see that she was not just still on her feet, but going about with renewed energy. He could only suppose that the events of the last half hour had caused some sort of brainstorm. Maybe it was time stop all this nonsense and find out what was going on.

He was about to drop the pipe when there was a sound like the death rattle of a Turkish tea urn and water shot out of it, all over his trousers. The shock jerked him upright so that he nearly let go altogether. He came out of his coma, stepped closer to the fire and started squirting water at it.

How long he stood there playing water over the blazing dresser, he could not say. All he knew was that, bit by bit, the water was getting the better of the fire until at last, with one astonished hiss, it was out. What remained was a charred mess but the damage was more to the dresser than the building.

'Stop!' Archie yelled as water continued to pour out of the pipe. He had to repeat this several times before the flow eventually reduced to a trickle then ceased altogether. He stood there, wondering what was going on and hoping he wasn't about to wake up and find it was all a dream.

'Well done, Archibald,' said his aunt, appearing round the corner. 'We'll have somewhere to sleep tonight after all.'

'Could I ask a question?'

'Of course, ask away.'

'How come I was able to squirt water from a hose in a house with no running water?'

'Ah that,' said Ruby. 'Not too difficult really when you have the right equipment.'

'Which is what?'

'It's called a stirrup pump.'

'A what?'

'A stirrup pump. They were used during the war, mainly by people called firewatchers. Their job was to keep watch during air raids. So if, for example, a fire-bomb fell on a building, it could be put out before it took hold and burned the place down.'

'Fascinating! So that's what you just used?'

'It was. Do you want to see it?'

'Of course.'

'Then give me the end of that hose and step this way.'

He trotted after her round the corner. There he saw that the other end of the hose was attached to a metal tube standing in a bucket of water.

'Here we go,' said Ruby, grasping a handle at the top of the tube and pumping it vigorously up and down. 'You just operate it like this, and you have a working hose.'

'So I see,' said Archie, just managing to dodge the stream of water that shot out of the end of the pipe. 'But what happens when the bucket is empty?'

Now that's the interesting bit,' said Ruby. The old firewatchers used to have a line of full buckets at the ready. We don't have that but what we *do* have, is the water butt.'

'The water butt?'

'Don't tell me you've never noticed it?'

Archie eyed the big old wooden barrel. 'Can't say I have. It's not one of the most memorable features around the place, is it?'

'It may not be that, Archibald, but it is one of the most useful. It collects and stores rainwater from the gutters, which is useful for the garden in dry weather.'

'And you use this gadget to spray it around?'

'Exactly. You place the bucket under the tap at the bottom of the butt, open it and *Hey Presto*, you have a continuous flow!'

'Wow! What a great idea!'

'The simple ideas are always the best, don't you think? Ready for a cup of tea?'

41

It was two days before Ruby and Archie felt able to relax. As they sat in the living room sipping tea, Ruby said, 'We were lucky!'

'But it wasn't just luck,' said Archie. 'That stirrup pump saved the day.'

'I meant it was lucky the pump was left in the outhouse. If it had been in the shed, it would have been burnt along with the rest.'

'Phew! I see what you mean.'

'And what's more,' said Ruby, now with the bit firmly between her teeth, 'if the fire had started anywhere but in the kitchen, we'd have lost the cottage.'

'Dare I ask why?'

'The kitchen was an addition to the original building, and it has a slate roof.'

'I obviously haven't been paying attention. You mean a fire anywhere else would have got into the thatch and that would have been goodbye Oak Tree Cottage.'

Ruby shuddered. 'That's right. It doesn't bear thinking about, does it? We've got to stop this maniac before things get any worse.'

'I agree Aunt Ruby, we can't keep relying on luck. A good thing the fire raiser didn't notice that slate roof.'

'Probably because he was in too much of a hurry.'

Two days after the fire, the mess had been cleared up, insurance reinstated and calm restored.

'I think I'll pay a visit to Al Richards, today,' said Archie. 'He may be able to throw some light on those notes of Fred's.'

'While you're out,' said Ruby, would you mind looking in the shops for me? 'I need a cupboard of some sort. The fire has made me short of storage space.'

'Okay,' said Archie. 'I'll have a look in that big second-hand shop before I see Al.'

'I don't want anything with woodworm,' said Ruby.

'I'm sure Al has no woodworm,' said Archie, reassuringly.

It was lunchtime in the Blue Barrel and Archie and Al Richards were at one of the tables.

'So, how can I help?' asked Al as they settled down.

'Have you ever heard about something called the Cora necklace?' said Archie.

'The Cora Necklace? Of course I have. It was all over the papers. It was actually a collection of jewellery, but the necklace was the main item. It was owned by Cora Bagshot, wife of a local businessman and it was stolen from the house one night nearly twelve months ago. Joe Bradley and a couple of our blokes had been doing some work on the house but they'd finished and left, two days beforehand. The police were baffled because there was no sign of a forced entry. A small bedroom window was left open but it was too small for a man to squeeze through.'

'So I believe. My aunt's been telling me all about it or, to be more precise, she's been telling me all about Fred's version of it.'

'I didn't know Fred was involved.'

'He wasn't. At least not officially. But because it took place on his patch, he started taking a close interest in it. In fact it seems he became quite obsessed with the case and had a theory that Bradley was behind it.'

'Well, Bradley was one of those questioned but it seems that on the night of the actual burglary, he was miles away,' said Al.

'Yes, but apparently Fred thought that the alibi was just a bit too neat. He was convinced that Bradley organised the burglary for somebody else to carry out.'

'And you believe that?' said Al.

'As a matter of fact, after a recent conversation, I know it to be true.'

Al raised his eyebrows. 'Really, so who did you have this conversation with?'

'I thought you'd ask me that,' said Archie, 'but I don't think I'll mention any names, just yet. But, if I do get proof, you'll be the first to know. You don't mind, do you?'

'Of course I mind,' said Al. 'I'm as nosey as the next fella. But I'll wait.'

'Thanks,' said Archie, 'but right now I have another question for you.'

'Oh, yes? Go on then.'

Archie produced the notebook. 'These are some of Fred's private notes I found in his old shed.' He pointed a finger at one of the entries. 'Does that mean anything to you?'

'JB-SP-Cora-Garage?' Al read out in a low voice. 'I dunno. What do *you* think it means?'

'I think it means that Fred thought Bradley's garage was a hiding place for stolen property. The Cora necklace certainly comes under that heading.'

'Well, that fits the shorthand, but it doesn't really matter now does it?'

'Why not?'

'Because that was then and this is now, twelve months later. If Bradley was involved in pinching the necklace, he's had plenty of time to get rid of it.'

'That would be true if he was a professional jewel thief, but he isn't.'

'So you think he's still sitting on it, wondering what to do next?'

'Yes, I did think that, until I had a look.'

'What do you mean, you had a look?'

'I looked in his garage. It's as clean as a whistle. If there was any stolen stuff in there, it's gone.'

Al gaped in astonishment. 'You're not telling me you broke into his garage?'

'Don't sound so surprised,' said Archie. 'I had some help. But, yes I did.'

'I don't know what to think. I'm gobsmacked.'

'Okay, so if you could unsmack your gob for a moment, do you agree that Fred's notes suggest that, at some point, stolen property was in the garage?'

'It certainly looks that way, although I suppose the "garage" bit could refer to his lock-up garage.'

'What lock-up garage?'

'The one near his yard.'

'Bradley has a garage in his yard?'

'Well not exactly *in* the yard. It's on the housing estate nearby.'

Archie banged the palm of his hand against the side of his head. 'I'm an idiot. Al. I never thought of that. I should have asked you in the first place.'

'You're not proposing to break into that one are you? I

wouldn't advise it. It's solid concrete and you'd need a big drill. Drills tend to be a bit noisy and especially at night when everything's gone quiet. Anyway, if he did have it in there once, I'm sure it's long gone by now. In spite of what you say, I think he'd have found a way of getting rid of it.'

'I'm not so sure about that,' said Archie. 'First, the jewellery would have to be broken up in some way to disguise its origins. Second, if he did try to sell it, they'd want to screw an obvious amateur like him for all they could get. And from what I know of Bradley, that wouldn't go down well. And third, to do all that, he'd have to have the sort of contacts that only the professionals have. So, it's possible he still has the necklace and is just biding his time. In the long run, he'd want money rather than keeping something to hang round his neck.'

'Very true,' said Al, 'it wouldn't suit him.'

42

In the lounge bar of The Highwayman, Maisie was attending to the usual crowd but with some help. The landlord, having recovered from his bout of flu, was doing his share of pint pulling. Archie was pleased to see Corky and the Major were in their usual places. Corky appeared to be his usual gloomy self, but the Major was looking decidedly chipper. They greeted him warmly.

'The next round is mine,' said Archie. 'I owe you one for the recent show of support.'

'On the contrary,' said the Major, 'I feel I owe you, otherwise I would never have met Sarah.'

'Sarah?'

'*The Echo* photographer. She produced those pictures for the trial, remember?'

Archie nodded. 'Of course! Without them, we'd have been in trouble. They clinched the case and I'm obliged to you Major. I'm also wondering how you did it. I tried to get her to bung me a few of the photos but in the end she turned me down. However, you succeeded where I failed. I wonder why?'

'Who knows, old boy? Maybe you were just not her type but more likely it's because I'm more in her age group. Anyway, whatever the reason, she and I just seemed to get on. In fact we've become quite close.'

'Very close I'd say,' said Maisie, who'd been earwigging nearby. 'I see you've shaved off the moustache, Major.'

'Yes, quite,' said the Major. 'Don't want any complaints on that score. Anyway, I hope to be moving out of the digs soon. Sarah and I are thinking of setting up an antiques business together. I know a bit about old firearms and she is *au fait* with pottery.'

'Wow!' said Archie enthusiastically, 'you certainly don't let the grass grow, Major. Anyway, good luck to you both. The usual all round Maisie, please.'

'I love it when the right people get together,' said Maisie, shooting Archie a warm glance.

'What about yer landlady?' said Corky, addressing the Major.

'What about her?'

'Well, she'll have nobody to moan at, will she?'

'Are you volunteering?' said Archie.

'No mate. I'm just saying.'

'She can always get another lodger,' said Archie. 'They could get on well if she picks the right one.'

'You mean someone more compatible?' said the Major.

'Exactly. Someone with even more complaints than she has,

would be good. They could compare notes.'

They were enjoying their drinks in the pleasant silence of good companionship when the door opened and in came Gino, accompanied by an icy blast. The atmosphere of bonhomie was soon dispelled as he crossed the floor, looking distraught.

'Gino!' said Maisie. 'Is something the matter?'

'You bet!' said Gino. 'I wanna talk to you.'

'Just me?'

'Mebbe Archie an' all.'

'Okay.' She looked over at the landlord, who nodded. 'Let's go in the back.'

In the back room, Gino looked as if he was about to burst in to tears. 'He gone!' he wailed.

Archie sought clarification. 'Who's gone and where?'

'Peppi, he gone!'

'Your monkey's missing?'

'No, he dead!'

Archie and Maisie looked at each other in shocked silence.

Archie took a breath. 'Tell us about it. How did it happen?'

'I get message, he got sick. I say to Bradley, Peppi, he needs me. He very sick. I gotta go.'

'And he refused?'

'Yeah, you right. He make me carry on working. By the time I get home Peppi is very ill. Mrs O'Hara, she goin' frantic. She don' know what to do.'

'Your landlady?'

'Yeah. Anyhow, I wrap Peppi in a blanket and take him to da vet's. But it too late. He already gone.' With that, the little man burst into sobs. 'He my best friend.'

'I'm sorry, Gino,' said Archie. He didn't know what else to say. He'd never been called upon to console someone for the loss of a monkey before.

Maisie put an arm round the little man's shoulders. 'I'm very sorry Gino,' she said. 'You have a lot of friends here. Can I get you something while you tell us what we can do?'

'No t'ank you, Maisie.' He wiped his eyes. 'Don' worry, I all right.' He suddenly had a hard look about him. 'That Bradley, he killed Peppi and I going to kill him.'

'Whoah!' said Archie, 'just take it easy. The authorities don't look kindly on settling differences that way and the days of pistols at dawn are over. Bradley may be an unfeeling crook but the best way to get at him is by making him answer for his misdeeds in a court of law.'

'Is dat so? Well I do anyt'ing. I ain't afraid of him no more. I give Peppi a good send-off, then I ready, okay?'

'Fine by me,' said Archie. 'He's earned it. After that, what we need is a good plan.'

43

Peppi was buried with due ceremony in a corner of the garden behind The Highwayman where he had done so much to entertain the clientele. When it was over, Gino, Maisie and Archie retired to the back room to discuss their next moves.

Gino was still rumbling on about seeing off Bradley one dark night, but he was vetoed by the others. 'We need something a good deal more subtle,' said Archie. 'I have an idea and I think it's time I took you into my confidence.'

Maisie seemed thrilled at the prospect of being Archie's *confidante*. They looked at him expectantly.

'The thing is,' said Archie, 'my previous suspicions about Joe Bradley hiding something in his garage have not entirely gone away. The trouble is that I've been looking in the wrong place. Apparently he has another garage near to his workshop.'

Gino nodded. 'Sure, I coulda told you dat.'

Archie eyed the little man with some slight disfavour. 'Well you might have said.'

'You shoulda asked.'

'Okay. Have you seen this garage?'

'O'course I have.'

Can it be broken into?'

'Not wit'out a bulldozer. Itsa concrete.'

'That's what I've been told. What about a key?'

'No chance. Bradley carries it always in his pocket.'

There was silence while Archie chewed this over. 'Okay,' he said finally, 'we'll have to get the police to look into it.'

'Sounds like a good idea,' said Maisie.

'The trouble is, they won't act on a mere suspicion and that's all I have at the moment. I have a suspicion but no proof.'

'How about an anonymous phone call?' said Maisie. 'I could do that.'

'I don't think so. They'd just think it was some joker trying to make fools of them.'

They looked at each other in bafflement. Finally Gino spoke up. 'Der's only one thing for it. I go in and tell them everyt'ink.'

Archie looked at him in astonishment. 'You can't do that. You'd be incriminating yourself.'

There was a silence as this sank in.

44

Ruby was reading the paper when she suddenly burst out, 'I don't believe it!'

Archie looked up. 'More gossip in *The Echo*?'

'Not gossip. This is under the heading of "Special Announcements". It's right after the "Births, Marriages and Deaths" column. So who do you think is engaged to be married?'

He considered. 'The only candidate who springs to mind is the Major, a friend I met in The Highwayman. He and someone called Sarah from *The Echo* have been seeing each other quite a lot recently.'

'No, it's not him. I'll give you three guesses.'

'I'm no good at guessing.'

'Well try.'

'Oh, all right. From the way you're asking, it must be someone unlikely. Let's see now. How about the unlovely trio of Sidney Burke, Charlie Leggit or Joe Bradley?'

Ruby looked a trifle miffed. 'How did you know?'

'How did I know what? Don't tell me it is one of those three?'

'It's Joe Bradley.'

'What!' Archie was dumbfounded for a moment. Then he remembered the letter he'd seen in the Bradley home. It had been positively littered with endearments such as 'Honeybunch'. If someone had said that to him, he wouldn't have believed it. But he'd read it with his own eyes.

'Well, I suppose anything's possible,' he said. 'Perhaps she met him in the dark. Are you quite sure about this?'

'I'm only telling you what it says here. Let me read it to you.'

She read from the page. 'Mr Charles FitzRobert of Barton Hall, Dunnerly is pleased to announce the engagement of his daughter Monica, to Mr Joseph Bradley, a building contractor of Priory Mount, Evesbury. A further announcement will be made when a date for the wedding has been arranged.'

'So she's the mysterious girlfriend,' said Archie.

'I didn't know he had a girlfriend.'

'Er, it has been rumoured.'

'I see. Well there's not much detail here, is there?'

'Maybe you should look elsewhere in the paper. It seems to have gone very gossipy lately.'

She nodded. 'You're right, they've started a column devoted to tittle-tattle.' She began turning the pages. 'Ah, here we are! Would you like me to read it to you?'

'Please do.'

'It says, "The engagement of Miss Monica FitzRobert to Mr Joseph Bradley (reported in the 'Special Announcements' column of this newspaper) will come as a great relief to her father, Charles FitzRobert, who owns and runs several big farms in the area. Apparently, he has been concerned recently about the lack of an eventual heir to his estate. Since he became a widower, his daughter, thirty-six year old Monica, has wanted to marry but there has been a marked lack of suitable candidates. This has been attributed to the fact she is extremely tall (over six feet, in fact). It seems that the search is now over".'

'That rings a bell,' said Ruby. 'I've heard about this girl of six feet something who can't find a tall enough boyfriend.'

'Well, she seems to have found one now,' said Archie. 'Bradley is a beanpole if ever I saw one. Her previous boyfriends must have decided that her wealth would not compensate them for having a permanent crick in the neck. But with Bradley, not only can he look her in the eye without the use of a stepladder, but having been expensively educated, he can play the part of the gentleman for all it's worth. It looks like he'll be in clover when actually he should be in jail.'

'My sympathies are all with Monica,' said Ruby.

At that moment there was a loud knock. 'Who can it be at this time?' wondered Ruby.

'Don't worry,' said Archie. 'I have this infallible method of finding out. It involves the opening of a door.'

On the doorstep, he saw a familiar figure. 'Major!' he said, 'what are you doing here?'

'Sorry to trouble you old boy,' said the Major, 'but I have some news that I think you should hear.'

'Well, don't stand there shivering,' said Archie. 'Come on in.'

Inside, Archie said, 'Aunt Ruby, I'd like you to meet Mike Chiselhurst, a friend of mine who's recently left the army.'

'Pleased to meet you,' said Ruby. 'You look cold. Why don't you sit by the fire?'

'Thank you,' said the Major, as he sat down. 'and *I'm* pleased to meet *you*. You are something of a legend down at The Highwayman.'

'Really?' said Ruby. 'So you've been talking about me have you, Archibald?'

'Only the good bits, Aunt. Not that there are any bad bits,' he added hastily.

'Would you like a cup of tea, Mr er ...'

'Please call me Mike. And yes, tea would be splendid.'

'Maybe a whisky would help to thaw him out better,' said Archie.

'Of course,' said Ruby, 'you can do the honours.'

'So what was this news you wished to impart, Major?' Archie enquired as he busied himself.'

'It's about this builder, Joe Bradley.'

Ruby snorted. 'Oh him! We've just been talking about him. He seems to have got himself in with a rich family. After the things he's done, he should be in jail.'

'Ah yes!' said the Major, 'that's what I came about.'

'We appreciate that, Mike,' said Archie. 'but actually we've read all about his engagement in *The Echo*.'

'Ah, yes. I'm afraid that story is a bit out of date. Sarah, my girlfriend, is still working as a reporter, though she is on her notice. The police keep the paper informed and according to the latest information, Joe Bradley has been arrested.'

Archie made an effort to prevent his jaw from dropping into the whisky glass. 'D'you know Major, I could have sworn you said Bradley had been arrested.'

'Exactly right,' said the Major. 'It seems our entertainer friend, Gino, went to the police and gave them the full story about Bradley's criminal activities, including his own part in it. As a result, they broke into Bradley's garage and found the stolen jewellery, hidden in a roof space.'

'Wow!' said Archie. 'Good old Fred. He was right all along.'

Ruby was goggling, robbed of speech, but only briefly. 'Who is this Gino?' she asked eventually.

'He sometimes entertains us at the Highwayman,' said Archie, but his day job is with Bradley. Unfortunately, Bradley has some sort of hold over him and forced him to pinch a valuable necklace. However, Gino obviously decided it was time to spill the beans.'

'What a hero!' said Ruby. 'After that, I think we all need a drink. Do you dance Mike?'

'I'm afraid not. These feet were made for marching.'

'Pity. I feel like waltzing round the room.'

'You waltz, we'll watch,' said Archie. 'Cheers everyone!'

45

The next day, Archie and Ruby were still chewing over the news of Bradley's arrest when there was another knock on the door. Once again it was the Major who stood on the step.

'Apologies for pestering you again, old boy,' he said. 'I'm not stopping but I thought you should know that there's been a further development.'

Archie opened the door wider. 'I'm all ears, Mike,' he said, 'but do come in and sit down.'

'I'm afraid I have an appointment,' said the Major. 'but I thought I should let you know that Charlie Leggit, the councillor, has also been arrested.'

'Wow!' said Ruby who had suddenly appeared at Archie's side. 'You are a bringer of good news. Do you know the reason?'

'Yes, apparently they found a ledger in Bradley's garage that shows a true account of his business dealings as opposed to the one in his office, which is for the benefit of the Inland Revenue. It shows several sums of money paid to a "C. Leggit" that they suspect are bribes.'

'So Leggit's been taken in for questioning?'

'Exactly. But the real reason I called is to tell you is that Leggit has been loudly protesting his innocence and making accusations against various different people. For instance, he claims that you threatened him with a shotgun, Mrs Manning. So it may be that the police will be round to ask questions and possibly take the gun away for evidence.'

'Ah,' said Ruby, 'I've no worries on that score. Fred renewed the firearms licence just before he, er, passed on. It's still valid.'

'That's good!' said the Major. 'Anyway, I thought I should just warn you. Now, if you don't mind, I really must dash.'

'Of course, Major,' said Archie with a grin, 'it wouldn't do to keep her waiting.'

After the Major had marched away, they went back inside. 'Are you sure about that licence, Aunt Ruby? It wasn't amongst the papers that were burgled was it?'

'No, it wasn't. I keep it in the cabinet with the gun.'

'What sort of a cabinet is it?'

'A gun cabinet, what else?'

'Do you keep it locked?'

'No, I don't.'

'I thought that was the law.'

'Well, Fred always kept it locked but I like to keep it handy for seeing unwelcome people off the premises.'

'And the odd nephew, of course.'

'Only when they disguise themselves in mud.'

'Touché. Can I have a have a look at the said weapon?'

'Of course.' Ruby went to the cupboard under the staircase and reached inside to produce the gun. 'There we are,' she said, 'it's in a handy place when it's wanted in a hurry. Let's take it into the kitchen. You can see better in there.'

In the kitchen, Ruby handled the old weapon carefully. 'There we are,' she said, 'Fred's pride and joy. He used it to keep down the rabbit population.'

Archie nodded. 'And you use it to keep down the unwanted visitor population.'

'Well, it seems to work better than just shouting at them.'

'Have you ever fired it?'

'No, Archibald, I've never fired it and I've no intention of doing so.'

'What about ammunition?'

'There is no ammunition. I gave the remaining cartridges to Bill Dobbs, the farmer up the road. There were two boxes of them as I remember.'

'Well, apart from keeping the cabinet locked, all that sounds good Aunt Ruby. I can't see there's much of a case to be made against you for threatening behaviour.'

'Of course not,' said Ruby. 'It's no threat to anyone. It may look threatening because I keep it in good shape, just as Fred used to do. A drop of linseed oil on the stock, a bit of grease round the working parts and it looks all ready to use.'

To demonstrate, she raised the gun to her shoulder, squinted along the barrel and pulled the trigger. There was a loud bang, a lump of plaster fell from the ceiling and dust drifted down on their heads. Ruby stood motionless in shock.

'Wow!' said a shaken Archie. 'Makes you wonder what would happen if it had been loaded.'

46

The trial at Evesbury Crown Court caused quite a stir in the town, on a par with the Annual Regatta or a visit from a VIP. When it began, the public gallery was overflowing with Ladies Club members, clientele from The Highwayman pub, members of the local Amdram group and other assorted nosey parkers.

The first of the accused to take the stand was Sidney Burke, accused of impersonating a council official in order to gain entry to private property. Sidney was beside himself with excitement at the prospect. It wasn't often he got to be the centre of attention, his role in the Amdram group having been confined to a few minor duties backstage. Now, here he was, with a starring role and a full house to go with it. He decided to take full advantage of the opportunity by dispensing with the services of a defence lawyer and taking on the role himself.

As noted previously, Sidney was a devotee of *Amazing Adventures*, a magazine that covered every kind of drama, including courtroom trials. These, he felt, had given him enough knowledge of legal proceedings, to take on his own case.

So, he launched himself on an unsuspecting court, striking a pose, thumbs hooked in the armholes of his waistcoat (bought specially for the occasion). He introduced himself with a lengthy exposition of the merits of English law until cut short by the Judge, who said, that if it was all right with him, he should stop waffling and get on with the defence.

Sidney, slightly miffed by this attitude, proceeded as requested and called his first witness. From there on, it all seemed to go downhill. Those who were asked to testify to Sidney's honesty and integrity, tended to hint that he was an apple short of a full barrel, whilst the prosecuting council decided that what they were hearing from witnesses, was doing a good enough job on its own without too much interference from them.

Eventually, the Judge took the unusual step of ordering the jury to ignore everything they'd heard, as Sidney would not be taking any further part in the trial, pending a psychiatric report.

Next up was Joe Bradley. His strategy was to say as little as possible on the grounds that anything he did say would tend to incriminate him. His lawyer portrayed Bradley as just a humble builder, trying to scrape an honest living in an uncertain world. Mr Bradley was, said the brief, baffled by the amount of red tape involved in getting the go-ahead to put up a few houses in an area that badly needed them. As for the jewellery in his garage, it could have been planted there by anyone and he particularly suspected Gino Conti, an ex-employee of his who seemed to have a grudge against him. The burglary, it was claimed, had nothing to do with him and he had the alibi to prove it. And as far as the accounts ledger was concerned, well that was just a practice exercise in bookkeeping and not to be taken seriously.

Meanwhile, Charlie Leggit had decided to pin his hopes on gaining the sympathy of the jury. He was disappointed to note that for the most part they looked a hard-nosed lot, but he'd spotted a lady in a fur hat at the front, who had a sympathetic look about her. While he couldn't actually talk to her, he felt he could project his innocent charm across the courtroom. He set about the task, and after a while felt sure she was responding to his meaningful gaze. This went on for some time until eventually the usher handed him a note asking him would he kindly refrain from ogling one of the jurors in that leering and offensive manner.

Gino was the only one of the accused to plead guilty and admitted to stealing a valuable necklace. He said he'd been made to do it by Joe Bradley who was blackmailing him over the matter of an expired visa. He was, he said, heartbroken over the loss of his pet monkey, an event for which he blamed Bradley, who he described not only as a thoroughly bad person, but an animal murderer into the bargain.

Danny Dooley, Bradley's hit man, was accused of starting a fire in Ruby's Cottage with intent to destroy it. He denied the charge but his case was rather undermined by the sight of the bandage round his burnt right hand.

Witnesses were called at various points including Ruby, who gave evidence in a clear and concise way, although (on Archie's advice) barely restrained herself from voicing her disgust of Bradley in graphic terms.

Constable Will Perkins of Evesbury police gave evidence regarding the shotgun owned by Mrs Manning. As the son of a farmer himself, he recognised a well-kept weapon when he saw one and reported that it appeared to be well-maintained and had even looked freshly cleaned when he collected it. He'd found the licence to be up-to-date and as there was no ammunition on the premises, he could not see how it could possibly be a threat to Councillor Leggit as claimed.

On the fourth day, the judge Mr Justice Crabtree summed up the evidence and instructed the jury to retire and consider their verdicts on each of the accused. They duly disappeared into the jury room but were back in less than an hour. As soon as the court had reassembled, the foreman announced a verdict of 'guilty' in all four cases.

The judge then thanked the jury for their efforts and announced that sentences would be passed on all four during the following week.

47

The morning sun lit up the kitchen as Ruby sat compiling her shopping list. She paused to wonder if salmon wouldn't make a nice change from her usual recipes. It was difficult to concentrate as her mind kept wandering back to the events of the previous few days. Her thoughts were interrupted when she heard Archie, back from his trip into town.

'Archie,' she called.

'Yes, Aunt?'

'Would you like a change of menu today?'

'Anything you put before me will be fine.'

'That doesn't answer the question.'

'Okay, it would help if you were to name a few alternatives.'

'Well, how about salmon then?'

'I love salmon.'

'Good. En croute?'

'On anything you like. And I have some news for you.'

'You have?'

'The judge has spoken and I know you've been waiting for news of the sentencing.'

'Hasn't everyone? So what happened?'

'Well, first Gino was sentenced to one year in jail. The sentence was suspended because of his cooperation with the police.'

'Good. I hope he'll he happy.'

'Then Dooley was given two years for his arson attack on the cottage.'

'He should have got more.'

'Leggit received three years for corruption and deception.'

'He should have got more too. So what about Bradley? And why are you giving me these in reverse order?'

'I thought it would make the results sound more exciting. You know, like announcing the winner of a beauty contest. And speaking of beauty, I'm taking Maisie to dinner tomorrow night.'

'Really? Well look before you leap, is the only advice I can offer.'

189

'Thank you Aunt, I'll bear that in mind.'

'Please do. Now get on with it and tell me about Bradley.'

'Of course. Oh, by the way, it turns out that The Meadow was sold illegally. It's protected by some ancient law covering grazing rights. The locals have the right to graze their sheep there, but nobody can put up buildings on it. As for ownership, that will probably revert to the council.'

'Really? Well, I can't remember seeing any sheep there.'

'Doesn't matter. The law is the law.'

'So Fred always used to say. Now, are you going to tell me or do you want to go hungry tonight?'

'Of course. Sorry to keep you in suspense, but there are two things. First, Bradley's engagement is off and second, the judge gave him nine years.'

'Really? And about bloody time too,' said Ruby.

www.ingramcontent.com/pod-product-compliance
Lightning Source LLC
Chambersburg PA
CBHW050402030726
47503CB00006B/1987